The Watch

A NOVEL BY JAMES DALRYMPLE

LIGATT
PUBLISHING

1ST Edition: June 1, 2006

Written by: James Dalrymple
                 jdalrymple@ligattpublishing.com
Editor: Gregory D. Evans
                 gregoryevans@ligattpublishing.com
Co-Editor: Sara Latini,
                 sara@house9road47.com
Layout & Cover: Farah Khan,
                 design@house9road47.com

Cover Photography:
Back: Linda Armstrong
Front: Frank Kebschull
Agency: Dreamstime.com

For book signing and personal appearances contact us at:
(866) 3-LIGATT or contactus@ligattpublishing.com.

For bulk purchasing please contact:
LIGATT Publishing
13428 Maxella Drive
Suite 293
Marina Del Rey, Ca 90292
(866) 3-LIGATT

Time does not change us.
It just unfolds us.

Max Frisch

CHAPTER ONE

THE MASSIVE WEB PRESSES OF THE SEATTLE TIMES press floor sucked an endless spool of once-white newsprint through a snake-like maze of steel gray machinery with a deafening roar somewhere just below the pain threshold. Seventy-one-year-old Elijah Spellman slowly maneuvered a push-broom down the rows of thundering belts, drums, pulleys, cutters, trimmers, and folders— oblivious to the mind numbing wail of the presses. His foam earplugs were snugly held in place by sound dampening ear pods, which creased his thinning gray hair. Eli, lost in thought, pushed a growing wall of paper shreds like a snowplow clearing a whitened street. This, Eli figured, was his 10,065th day of work at the Seattle Times. It was also his last

"Eli!" A shout carried on the breeze created by the streaming paper.

Mechanically, Eli plowed his way around the corner of the monstrous web press, trailing bits of paper against the edges of the machinery. "Good riddance", he thought. "I can finally do what I want." He stopped pushing and stared blindly into the blurred paper racing past. "What am I going to do?"

Leaning against the broom handle, he looked more closely at his gnarled hands. Age spots covered the peaks and valleys of veins and sinews like craters cover the surface of the moon. "I'm old," Eli thought matter-of-factly. "I'm too damn old to do what I want. And too damn tired." Flexing his arthritic fingers, he curled them around the broom handle and set off to plow more paper.

"Eli!" The shout grew louder.

As he pushed the paper scraps around, thoughts of his barren, second-floor studio apartment filled his mind. Eli lived alone. He lived in a bad part of town. He rode the bus to work. He rode the bus home. He ate a bowl of cold cereal with toast for breakfast. He ate a grilled cheese sandwich for dinner. His *kitchen* consisted of a tiny refrigerator, a toaster, and the hot-plate he used for *grilling*. Near the window, a card-table-dining-set overlooked the dirty pavement of 1st Avenue's low-rent district. A small TV, rabbit ears included, rested against a barren wall in front of a worn out La-Z-Boy and a metal floor lamp. No need for any other furniture. Eli never had visitors.

"Elijah!"

The paper scraps were always there. As the speeding streams of paper raced through the press, shifting paper tension would create horizontal movement in the stream. When the paper streams got too close to the edges, paper shreds would fly from the press. The computer controlled paper tension would correct itself and the process would repeat to the other side. "Job security", Eli thought. Then he scowled. "I hate this job."

"Eli".

A hand reached out and grabbed Eli by the shoulder. He jumped, startled from his treasonous thoughts.

"Manuel!" Eli's heart thumped in his throat. He removed his ear pods, cringing as the web-grinding drilled his brain.

"Eli, you're done. Shifts over, man." 27 year old Manuel Ortega tugged at the broom handle firmly clenched in Eli's bony fingers.

Breathing just a little heavy, Eli slowly released the broom to Manuel's custody.

Smiling, Manuel took the broom and began to sweep. "Boss wants to see you on the way out."

Eli's hands and arms slowly fell to his side. The trails he had just swept were covered again with a layer of new fallen paper. He watched Manuel sweep the same row he had just finished plowing, then turned and left the press floor behind.

* * *

Eli sat quietly in 25 year-old Don Morgan's birch wood paneled office. Don had been Eli's boss for about 6 months. Don had come to work for the Times, right out of Seattle Pacific University. To Eli, Don was a smart-aleck kid. He was always in a hurry. Eli was annoyed to have to wait.

Footsteps echoed in the hallway as Don strode into the office, manila envelop in hand and sat down behind his desk in a large faux leather chair. Don, smiling rather lamely, held out a Styrofoam cup to Eli.

"Want a drink of cider," he said. Lifestyle section's doing a feature on the Fall Harvest Festival. Pretty good stuff."

"No thanks," Eli answered tersely. He was in no mood for 'socializing' with this 'kid'. He knew what this meeting was about. He also knew that no one really cared.

Failing to make eye contact with Eli, Don reached over and took a letter from his "out box", and began to read, "The Seattle Times would like to thank you for your unprecedented 40 years of service. Your punctuality and attendance record are an inspiration to us all."

Eli frowned, familiar scowl lines deepening across his forehead. Don continued.

"In token of our appreciation for your outstanding service, the Seattle Times would like to present you with this retirement package." Don reached across the desk and handed the manila envelope to Eli. "Inside the envelop, you will find the helpful and informative pamphlets titled, 'Accessing your 401k plan', 'Social Security—How to claim your benefits', 'A Seniors Guide to Retirement', 'Medicare–Secure Horizons', and, 'Retirement—Those Active Golden Years'."

With an air of contempt, Eli tore open the envelope and looked inside for his very own copies of these helpful and informative brochures. Don, seeming to swell with pride, reached into his desk drawer, and pulled out another envelope. He continued to read.

"In addition to your retirement information, the Seattle Times would like you to have, as a small token of our appreciation, this bonus check for $250, a gift certificate to Sizzler, and a vintage gold pocket watch."

Don handed the envelope to Eli and looked up, smiling. Eli took the envelope and looked inside, expectantly.

Don smiled a little bigger and nodded his head.

The envelope, the gift certificate, and even the check were tokens. He had worked at the company for 40 years. He, unlike most people, had gradually worked his disappointing way down the corporate ladder of success.

No one in the present company could remember the days Eli worked as an Engineer, designing ways the company could put out ever increasing numbers of papers. No one remembered his days as a pressman, nursing and cajoling a temperamental hot type press into outputting another *special edition*. Now, he was a press floor maintenance man. A custodian. "Thank you very much for your 40 years. Here's 250 bucks. Take your spouse to dinner at Sizzler." Hell, he didn't even have a spouse.

"Where's the watch?" Eli asked.

Don's smile held, with effort. "Usually, Mr. Blethen presents the watches. I sent a memo to HR informing them of your retirement. I thought he'd be here."

"Mr. Blethen?" Eli asked incredulously.

"That's right," Don returned.

"Alden Blethen?"

"Yes," Don's lips stuck to his dried out teeth. His tongue snaked out to moisten them.

"Alden J. Blethen, the company founder?"

"Yes!"

Eli stood up to leave. He always knew he wouldn't get the 'steak or chicken' retirement party. But he was hoping to get the 'gold watch'. Not now.

"Blethen's dead!" Eli said.

Don jumped up from his leather chair.

"His son, Eli. I mean his son." Don rushed around the desk.

"Right." Eli turned and walked out the office door.

"Wait Eli. I'll call HR. We'll get your watch."

"Forget about it. I don't have time."

"Eli. Eli Spellman!" An old man, older and more weathered than Eli, called out from down the office corridor, in a raspy sort of voice.

Eli stopped.

"Mr. Blethen!" Don called back. "Boy am I glad you're here."

The old man hobbled closer. "Looks like a homeless guy," Eli thought.

"I have arrived just in time," Blethen put out his hand to Eli.

Eli gripped Mr. Blethen's wrinkled fingers, and shook. "He's pretty strong, for an old guy," Eli thought.

"It's a pleasure to meet you sir," Eli said.

"The pleasure is all mine Mr. Spellman. I have heard a great deal about you over the years."

The color rose in Eli's cheeks. He couldn't decide whether this old guy was crazy, or just making fun of him.

"I hope it was all good," Eli said.

"Mostly," Blethen answered, with a wry smile.

Eli smiled back. "Good answer." He liked this guy. "He must be 90," Eli thought.

"97, to be exact," Blethen said.

"What?" Eli said.

"97. I'm 97 years old today."

"Happy birthday," Eli said.

"Why, thank you young man," Blethen said, with a twinkle in his eye.

Don looked puzzled. Eli laughed out-loud. It wasn't very often that he was called a 'young man'.

Alden Blethen placed his hand on Eli's shoulder and guided him into Don's office. Don wagged behind.

"Sit down Eli. I have a gift for you," Mr. Blethen sat in the stiff office chair next to Eli. Eli sat down uncomfortably.

"Thank you, sir. But I really do have to go. I have to make the 5:30 bus."

"Plenty of time," Blethen said. "Now, for this gift."

Mr. Blethen leaned back in the chair to gain access to his pants pocket. He placed his hand in his pocket and extracted a gold pocket watch.

"A long time ago, my Father purchased a number of these watches. He gave me one much like this. Each watch was specially inscribed. This watch is for you, Eli Spellman."

Mr. Blethen looked Eli directly in the eye and held out the watch. Eli looked backed at Mr. Blethen, and then down at the watch.

"Go on Eli. It's yours. Read the inscription."

Alden Blethen opened the gold cover, revealing the crystal face. He placed the watch gently in Eli's hand.

When the watch touched his skin, Eli felt something. The room shifted. Dizzy. Something. Eli touched his temple. His head hurt.

Blethen didn't seem to notice.

"Etched inside the watch are the words, 'To Elijah Spellman. Time does not change us. It just unfolds us.'"

"Did Blethen read those words, or did I?" Eli thought.

He stared at the watch. He read the quote again. "Time does not change us. It just unfolds us."

Somewhere, down deep, Eli felt like it was a lie. He knew he had changed. He felt all folded up inside. But, he longed to be 'unfolded'.

Eli continued to stare at the watch, through the watch, his eyes losing focus.

Gradually Eli became aware that the only sound in the room was the ticking of the black and white wall clock. How long had he been sitting there. He couldn't tell. Was it an eternity, a lifetime, or just a moment? He couldn't tell. Did it really matter anyway? He'd never be back. This was it. This is what it felt like. Forty years. Forty years. And now, after all this time, he had his gold watch. He looked up from the watch, his eyes slowly focusing.

"Is there anything I can do for you?" Don spoke, somewhat worried.

Eli started. "What?"

"Is there anything I can do for you? Do you need a ride or something?"

"Where's Blethen?"

"Who?" Don looked puzzled.

"Mr. Blethen—Alden Blethen—the watch."

Don looked at his wristwatch, and stood up. Meeting over.

"Look, Eli, if you need a ride or something I could have one of the guys give you a lift."

Eli stared at the young man behind the desk, young enough to be his grandson. That is, if he had had any children, let alone, grandchildren. His wife died in a car accident, on their honeymoon. Eli never remarried.

"No, thanks," Eli said.

Don shuffled around his desk and stuck out his hand. "Thanks Eli. It's been great bein' yer boss. I've learned a lot from you."

Eli carefully closed the cover of the intricately engraved gold watch—his watch, and lifted himself out of the chair with great effort. Don's handshake was weak and flimsy. Eli's was still strong. Don winced.

"What?" Eli asked.

"What, what?" Don pulled his throbbing fingers free.

"What did you learn from me?" Eli's gaze demanded an answer.

"Uh… well… uh… you were always on time." Don freed himself from Eli's gaze and made for the office door.

"Yeah right. I was always on time". Eli had just been dismissed. After forty years, he had been dismissed. He thought, "For your sake, it was just in time."

Don's lame smile returned. "Well then… good luck. See you around."

"Yeah. See you around."

Eli stepped past Don, into the hallway. He put his 'bonus check' and gift certificate inside the manila envelop and placed the newly treasured golden watch in his pocket. Don watched uncomfortably as Eli wrapped himself in a worn out London Fog overcoat and trudged out of the office into the steel gray sky of a September afternoon in Seattle.

CHAPTER TWO

THE TIMES PLANT WAS LOCATED at the north end of Elliott Bay, right on the waterfront. Eli needed to walk two blocks east, up a steep hill to get to the bus stop on 1st Avenue, that would take him to his lonely apartment. His apartment was only a few miles away, but it took the bus nearly 45 minutes to travel the distance. The bus stopped every 30 minutes. He hated to miss the 5:30 run.

Eli stepped off the curb and crossed the street, beginning the steep climb up Ivar Street. The old red brick buildings of the downtown waterfront district watched his ritual passing for the last time. A stiff breeze funneled between the buildings, carrying moisture off the bay and giving Eli a gentle push, up the hill. Winded from the steep climb, Eli stopped to rest under a side street coffeehouse awning. His heart was beating, way too fast, he thought. He turned his collar up against the wind. Looking back at the Times building below, he thought, not about his forty years of work there, but about the white caps breaking against the wind on Elliot Bay, beyond. "It's going to rain," he thought. Gray clouds were rolling in, over the water. Squalls were already visible, streaking the sky a darker gray. He pulled the golden watch from his pocket and opened the face. 5:21. Nine more minutes to go one more block. One more block. Straight up.

Eli gently put the watch back in his pocket and continued the final ascent to 1st Avenue. Step, step, step. He thought, "keep your feet moving." Like a mountain climber ascending the last hundred feet of Mount Everest, Eli placed one foot after another, slowly, methodically, mechanically, almost incoherently.

Triumph. He crested the hill and reached the corner of Ivar and 1st. Bending at the waist and wheezing to catch his breath, he thought, "don't have to do that again." A gust of wind chilled the beads of sweat dripping from his forehead. Straightening a bit, he looked for the bus. A plump woman in a gingham dress, thick sweater, brown boots and an umbrella watched the color drain from his face.

"Late, as usual", she smiled warmly.

Eli breathed, unable to completely catch his breath. "Figures."

"These hills are sure somethin'. I'm from the mid-west originally. Flat. Flat.

Flat. I tell you. I've been in Seattle now for 6 months. I still can't get used to it."

Eli's heart seemed to beat behind his eyeballs. The incessant pounding nearly drowned out the woman's mid-western twang. He tried, out of politeness to follow her conversation.

"I work in the WAMU building up the street. WAMU. That's short for Washington Mutual. But, I suppose you know that, bein' from Seattle and all. You are from Seattle aren't 'cha?"

Eli tried to nod and smile, reeling from the pounding in his head.

"I knew it. I can just tell when someone's a native Seattlite. You know, web-feet. Mossy toes. The Emerald city." She laughed at her own jokes.

Whooooosh. The air brakes of the 5:30 bus blew street trash and dirt into the air, mercifully interrupting the woman's monologue. The bus door sighed open and a few grunge rockers hopped off to a look of disdain from the woman.

"Well, there ya go. The bus is here. Would you like some help? You look like you could use some help."

The woman took Eli by the elbow and pushed him at the bus. "Would you like me to sit by you?"

"No. No thank you. I'll be fine." Eli resisted the woman's help, and climbed up the bus steps. He dropped his tokens in the slot and started towards the back.

"Suit yerself. Did you see those two young men that just got off the bus? What is this world comin' to? I have never seen such hair color... "

The woman's voice continued to drone as Eli moved to the back. Gratefully, she took a seat near the front. Eli collapsed in a seat, alone. He took out his pocket watch and looked, 5:42. He should be home by 6:15.

* * *

The City Bus groaned to a painful stop. Eli pulled out his watch. 6:23. Late. The bus doors coughed open and Eli stood up. A painful rhythm pounded in his head, synchronized to the fading boombox beat as a couple of kids jumped off the bus into a cold drizzle. An old woman stepped onto the bus, her overcoat and umbrella shedding water on the steps and aisle. Eli made his way forward. Slowly. It felt to Eli like the bus had not come to a complete stop. It seemed like the bus was going around a sharp corner, much too fast. Eli stopped and held on, waiting for the bus to straighten out.

"You comin' or goin'?" The large black bus driver turned around, hollering at Eli.

"Goin,'" Eli called back feebly.

"Then get your butt off my bus. I've got a schedule here."

"Since when?" Eli muttered as he struggled forward.

"Don't mess with me old man." The bus driver had heard his comment.

"Watch yer step."

Eli held the front step rail with one hand, his watch in the other. It seemed like an awfully long way down. "Why was it so far down today?" He thought, vertigo whitening his knuckles on the handrail. Beads of sweat on Eli's forehead matched the beads of water on the bus windows.

"Today!" The bus driver barked.

One step. Two steps. Eli looked down at the street. The wet pavement shone brightly as headlights from passing cars dizzyingly pierced the lowering gloom. Eli let go and stepped off. His right foot fell short of the curb, landing in the swiftly moving gutter stream. The world, it seemed to Eli, began to swirl in the vortex created by his worn out shoe. His left foot never found sure footing. Eli crashed to the ground, his left shin striking the edge of the curb. His right hand, fingers still clutching his precious gold watch, punched the sidewalk with Eli's full weight. A blinding flash of light filled his vision as his head met the cement.

Distantly, he heard a woman scream.

Someone yelled, "call 911."

"My watch," Eli thought.

"Call 911."

"My watch," he muttered out loud.

"Don't move," someone said.

"Get a blanket."

"Get him out of the rain."

"Are you O.K.?"

"Call 911. Has anybody called 911?"

"My watch," Eli croaked again.

Eli pulled his right hand out from under his body, into his field of vision. The skin of his knuckles was bloody from the fight with the pavement. But, he still had his watch. Slowly, his thumb pressed the latch on top of the watch. The watch didn't open as it had. He pried the cover open with his thumb and forefinger. The glass was broken. The hands were bent. The face was damaged.

"ARE YOU OKAY."

"My watch." Eli answered.

Drops of moisture fell from the sky. Drops of moisture fell from the corners of his eyes. Eli's vision and consciousness blurred to white as he stared at the broken face of his precious gold watch.

CHAPTER THREE

"ARE YOU OKAY?"

A bright light shone in Eli's eyes. It hurt. He closed his eyes tight.

"Elijah, can you hear me?" A soft, woman's voice caressed his mind.

His head hurt. His leg hurt. His hands hurt. His back hurt.

"Grandpa, wake up."

An engine rumbled, then died. A heavy door shut. Footsteps padded nearer. Whispers floated on a gentle breeze.

"Mom, what happened?"

"Maggie."

"Thank you so much for coming."

"Get back now child. Give me some room."

Eli could hear leather rustling, and a zipper opening.

"Elijah, can you hear me?"

Eli lay there.

Where?

He breathed in thick scents of cut grass. No, not cut grass, new mown hay, mixed with a sweet scent he didn't recognize. Rich dirt. The ground. It felt damp, cool, soft. A farm. His father's farm? "I must be dead", Eli thought. "I'm back on my father's farm." Birds were chirping softly and water was babbling nearby.

"Oh please Grandpa. You can't be dead." A child's voice whimpered.

"Hush up now child."

Eli twitched as a pain shot through his leg. "Ouch," his mind called out. "Ouch!" Again. The pain moved. His arm. "Stop that!" Something was poking and prodding. If I'm dead, how come it hurts so much. "Let me rest," he thought.

Leather rustled. The air vanished.

"Can't breath! It burns! My eyes! Stings!"

Eli gasped a great breath and called out, "Aoouuuuu!" He sat up, trying to breathe.

"Hold on there now Old Man. It's just the salts." Doc Jones, sixty-six and weathered, held Eli's shoulders in his old, but powerful hands.

Eli rubbed his eyes, and tried to struggle free.

"Not so fast. You've had a pretty bad fall," Doc Jones said.

Eli's head was spinning. Where was he?

Seven-year-old Emily 'Emy' Spellman, long blonde hair streaming behind, flew to her Grandfather.

"Grandpa! You're alive."

Eli winced as Emy's tiny bear hug compressed his bruised body.

"Not so hard Emy, Grandpa's hurt." Forty-six-year-old Thomas Spellman helped Doc Jones treat Eli.

"Come here Emy. Let Doc Jones do his work." Kneeling behind Doc Jones, sixty-six-year-old Maggie Spellman wiped her eyes with a bandana and gathered Emy in her flowing skirts.

"Who the hell are you people and where-in-the-hell am I?" Eli spat.

"Grandpa, you shouldn't swear," Emy answered.

"And you respect your Elders young lady," Thomas said.

Doc Jones swabbed a large cut on Eli's forehead.

"Ouch!" Eli cried and swatted at Doc's ministrations. "Who are you, and what am I doin' here?" Eli asked again.

Maggie held Emy a little closer. Tom looked at Doc Jones carefully. Their eyes met. Doc Jones looked back at Eli and just went on like things were normal, daubing the blood still trickling down Eli's forehead.

"You've had a bad fall Elijah. Hit your head a good one," Doc Jones said, as he began stitching the gash in Eli's forehead.

Eli winced, as the needle closed the gash.

"Hold still," Doc Jones said.

Eli looked around, for the first time. He was surrounded by trees. Apple trees. Apple trees loaded with apples. Rich, red, heavy delicious apples. The late afternoon sun shone through the thick orchard trees in speckled patterns, dancing on a gentle breeze. Three feet away, an old wooden stepladder lay on its side. A large wooden basket was tipped on its side, with several dozen apples strewn nearby. A plump, yet attractive older woman he didn't recognize knelt behind the man called Doc Jones. The woman held a pretty little blond girl around the waist. Another man, much younger and stronger, knelt beside Eli, holding him upright. The sense of peace and serenity in this place was strong. Just like his Father's farm. "It can't be," he thought.

The peace vanished. Eli began to breathe hard. Something was not right. "How did I get here? Who are these people? What happened to me?" The thoughts began to flood his mind. His head hurt.

"Listen here. I don't know who you people are, or how I got here. But I want some answers. NOW!" Eli struggled to get up. Thomas held him down. Doc Jones continued stitching.

"Calm down Elijah, it's alright," Maggie said.

"Let go 'a me. NOW!" Eli could feel panic rising in his chest. These people were trying to kidnap him. Rob him. "My watch," he thought.

"My watch! Where's my watch?"

Eli began to thrash his legs. Doc Jones knelt down on his thighs.

"Hold him tight Tom. I'm almost done. Maggie, get his feet," Doc Jones rasped.

"Get back child." Maggie pushed Emy away, as she grabbed hold of Eli's ankles.

Eli tried to throw a punch at the younger man holding him. Tom bear-hugged him around the chest, pinning his arms to his sides.

Even though he had just turned 71, Eli was still pretty tough. He knew he could get out of this, if he could... JUST... BREAK... FREE.

With a tremendous effort, Eli kicked, and straightened, and punched and flexed and the two men and one woman holding him lost their grip. Eli was on his feet in an instant. He had to run. He had to get out of there.

Maggie screamed.

"Grandpa, NO!" Emy called.

Eli looked back.

Two desperate steps and Tom was on him, tackling him to the ground. He hit his head. Everything went white.

The familiar scents were back. He couldn't see anything but white. Where was he? Voices floated on the gentle breeze.

"Damn it Eli. Now I'm gonna half to clean out that cut and re-stitch it."

A bee stung him in the shoulder. "Ouch," he thought.

"There. That should do it. He's not gonna wake up for a while."

"What's wrong Doc? How come he don't remember who we are?"

"... pretty bad bump... "

"... love you Elijah... "

"... small stroke maybe... "

"... love you Grandpa... "

The voices soothed his troubled mind. The voices faded. The scent of apple cider wafted through the air. "My watch," he whispered. But, he couldn't tell if he said it out loud, or just thought about it, as he drifted through the orchards of his father's farm.

CHAPTER FOUR

WHEN ELI WOKE UP, HIS WHOLE BODY HURT. "What a nightmare," he thought. "I'd better get moving or I'll be late for work. What time is it anyway?"

"Time?"

"Watch! Where's my watch?"

Eli sat up abruptly and called out, "Where's my watch?"

Where was he? This wasn't his room. His head started to spin and he collapsed back into the bed. The bed was big, bigger than Eli's single bed. A down comforter practically swallowed him up. Eli tried to grab hold of something to keep the room from spinning. Material. Sheets. Pillows. Eli was drowning in an endless sea of bed linen.

Slowly Eli felt the room begin to slow down. With the exception of an old looking wicker ceiling fan, spinning slowly above his head, Eli felt like the room had come to rest.

"Good morning sleepy head." Maggie stepped cheerfully through the bedroom door, carrying a breakfast tray. "Are you hungry?"

Suddenly Eli's stomach growled. He hadn't eaten since lunch yesterday, at the Times. Or was it yesterday? He wasn't sure where, or when he was.

"Where's my watch?" Eli said.

Maggie brought the breakfast tray over to the bed and sat down on the edge. The smell of home cooked food nearly overwhelmed him. Eggs, scrambled with cheese, four strips of bacon, three link sausages, two pieces of toast with strawberry jam, a slice of cantaloupe, a small glass of apple cider and a glass of whole milk. He hadn't eaten like this since he was a boy... on his father's farm.

"Emy found it by the tree, where you fell. She'll be over to see you in a few minutes. Sit up a bit, so I can spread this wrap out."

Obediently, Eli adjusted his body up against the carved oak headboard, large soft pillows scrunching behind him for support. Maggie tenderly placed a quilted shoulder wrap over the down comforter covering Eli's lap, and placed the breakfast tray on top. Absently, she picked up a piece of toast and took a bite, sampling her own strawberry handiwork, for taste. As she put the toast back on the tray, Eli noticed, for the first time, that his work shirt was missing. He had nothing on, but a T-shirt and boxers. Self consciously, he pulled the comforter up a little higher on his chest, nearly spilling the milk and cider.

"Careful, Sweetheart. I just changed the bedding yesterday," Maggie said softly.

"Who are you? What do you want? Where am I?" Eli spoke in rapid fire, still holding the comforter defensively.

Maggie looked down at the tray, not wanting Eli to see the hurt in her eyes.

"Just eat Elijah. Emy's gonna be here any moment. So's Doc Jones. He'll figure this whole thing out." Maggie sighed.

Eli could see the pain his questions caused this woman. But why? She was obviously sincere in wanting to care for him. But why again? She was pretty, in a down-to-earth sort-a-way. Eli noticed the crows-feet around her eyes and the smile lines of her rosy cheeks. She had deep green eyes that seemed to speak a lot more than she actually said, and Eli felt strangely drawn to her.

"Just answer me one question then," Eli said.

"Alright," she said carefully.

Eli watched her. She seemed… vulnerable. Scared, maybe. He reached out to the tray and picked up the glass of apple cider and took a drink. The liquid was sweet, and smooth, and quenching, and Eli closed his eyes as he felt its coolness all the way down his throat. He set the glass back on the tray and looked up.

"Who are you?" he asked.

Maggie looked up shyly, and their eyes met, hers moistening noticeably.

"I'm your wife Eli," she whispered.

For Eli, in that moment, time stopped. He was not aware of the morning sounds. He couldn't hear the ceiling fan rattling rhythmically, above him. He was lost, deep, in her eyes. Those eyes. Piercing green eyes. Familiar. Life giving. Loving green eyes. What could he be in those eyes? Who was he, in those eyes? How long had he known peace in those eyes? How long? How long?

"My watch!" he thought.

"Grandpa!" Emy Spellman burst into the bedroom with unstoppable enthusiasm. "Grandpa, you're all better." She ran to the bed.

"Slow down Honey," Maggie said, smiling.

Emy climbed up on the king size bed and snuggled in next to Eli.

"I love bacon," she drooled.

"Help yourself," Eli said, bewildered.

"Thank you Grandpa," Emy crooned, snatching a strip of bacon from the tray and munching it rapidly.

"Don't they feed you around here?" Eli said, as Emy munched away at the bacon strip.

Maggie laughed. "You can't keep this'n fed for love nor money."

Emy grabbed a link sausage with her fingers and began to munch it.

"Here's your watch Grandpa. You dropped it when you fell," Emy munched, as she set the watch on the nightstand.

"Don't talk with your mouth full, Sweetheart," Maggie corrected.

"Knock, knock." Doc Jones appeared in the doorway. Eli held on to the watch.

Maggie stood up, smoothed her skirted apron, and brushed back her graying hair. "Doc Jones! Come in. Eli was just having some breakfast. Although, Emy's had more than Eli. Emy come down off that bed."

"Mornin' Maggie. Emy," Doc Jones chuckled warmly, "Looks pretty good. Mind if I have some Elijah?"

"Why not, everybody else has," Eli frowned.

Doc Jones picked up a piece of bacon and began to eat. The truth be told, bacon was Eli's favorite. He picked up a piece and began to munch it himself. He didn't want to miss out entirely on this breakfast feast. He was hungry.

Maggie smiled with satisfaction. "Come with me Emy. Let Doc Jones do his work."

"Bye Grandpa," Emy said, scurrying out the door.

"Call me, if he gets too rough," Maggie said with a wink and a smile as she left the room.

Doc Jones and Eli watched her go. As she left, the room seemed, to Eli, to grow just a little dimmer.

Doc Jones finished munching his piece of bacon and set his black leather bag on the bed.

"So how are we this morning Elijah?" Doc Jones said, unzipping his black bag and taking a stethoscope out.

"I don't know how you are, but I'm having one hell-of-a bad dream, and I want some answers," Eli said getting angry.

"Deep Breath," Doc Jones said, placing the stethoscope on Eli's chest, and listening.

"Let it out."

"You gonna give me some answers, Doc?"

"Deep Breath," Doc Jones moved the stethoscope.

"Let it out."

"Well?" Eli said.

"Lean just a bit forward. There! Breath in." Doc Jones placed the stethoscope on his back.

"Let it out."

"Who are these people, and where am I?" Eli said, frustration rising.

"Calm down Elijah. Eat your breakfast. Give me your left arm." Eli set his watch down on the nightstand as Doc felt for his pulse.

Eli took a bite of the now cool scrambled eggs.

Doc Jones listened and counted silently. "Heart rate's a bit elevated."

"Damn it, Doc. What's goin' on? Where am I?"

Doc Jones released Eli's arm. "What's the last thing you remember, before you fell?" Doc Jones began changing the bandages on Eli's head.

Eli exhaled. "I was on my way home. From the Times. My last day. It was raining. I had a bad headache. I was getting off the bus. I missed the curb."

"You must have hit your head harder than I thought," Doc mused, finishing the bandage.

"What are you saying?" Eli flared.

"Eli, I've known you for 50 years. I've been your Doctor for 45. I delivered your kids. Our kids grew up together. I stayed with you and Maggie when Sarah had scarlet fever. I cried when Tom and Wilma lost little Eli, and I couldn't do a thing about it. I set your leg when you fell 15 years ago. You've been growin' apples in this valley all your life. Your father grew apples here. His father grew apples here. You've got a lifetime of memories here. You fell off the ladder picking apples with little Emy and hit your head. What in the sam-hill are you talkin' about? The Times? Getting off the bus? I need to get you into my office and have your head examined."

Eli set the breakfast tray aside and threw off the covers. "I'm gettin' outta here." He jumped out of bed. "Where're my clothes?"

Doc Jones stood up. "Take it easy Eli. You've got a concussion, coupled with a severe hematoma. You need to take it easy for a few days."

Eli pulled open the walk-in closet door. "Where are my clothes?"

On one side of the cedar lined closet were women's clothes. On the other side, men's clothes. He grabbed a Pendleton wool plaid shirt and put it on. It fit perfectly. He grabbed a pair of Levi's hanging on a hook and put them on. They fit just fine. He grabbed a pair of work boots from under a shelf and stormed out of the closet.

"I need some socks!"

"Sit down Eli, or I'm going to have to sedate you." Doc Jones pulled a syringe out of his bag.

Eli pulled open the upper right drawer of an oak dresser. He grabbed a pair of white cotton socks and sat down on the edge of the bed to put them on. "Leave me alone Doc! You're the crazy one."

Doc Jones jabbed the syringe into Eli's upper arm. Eli took a swing at him, and missed.

"It's for your own good Eli." Doc Jones pulled the syringe out of Eli's arm.

Eli swung at him again, slower, the drug instantly taking effect. "My name's Elijah Spellman. I live on first avenue south in Seattle, jus' before da viaduct." Eli tried desperately to hit his captor. Doc Jones was too fast for him.

"Why are you doin' this to me? Whadda you wan' from me?" Eli slurred.

"Rest Eli." Doc Jones held Eli's arms and sat him down on the bed. The drug took all resistance out of him. "It'll all be clearer in a little while," Doc said, as he pulled off Eli's boots and helped him lie down.

"What time is it?" Eli whispered.

Doc Jones looked at his watch. "It's about 9:30. Why?"

"My watch." Eli reached out for his gold watch. Doc Jones followed his reach and noticed the watch on the nightstand. He picked it up and looked at it.

"It's broken," Doc said.

Eli grabbed Doc Jones' wrist. "I want my watch!"

Doc Jones placed the gold watch in Eli's hand. Eli collapsed back into the softness of the pillows. His hand closed tightly around the gold watch. Tenderly, Doc Jones pulled the down comforter up around Eli's chin, as Eli's eyes closed.

CHAPTER FIVE

TWO LARGE COPPER KETTLES rested atop an old stove, gently steaming a humid aroma of boiling apples. Two apple pies baked in the oven just below, filling the Spellman country kitchen with the sweet smell of apple cinnamon. The apple harvest had begun, and the kitchen was a flurry of activity and conversation. Spellman women knew how to make use of apples. Apples in all their varieties. Apple sauce. Apple butter. Apple pie. Apple crisp. Apple cake. Apple cider.

Maggie, covered with flour, rolled out pie crusts with a heavy wooden rolling pin. Sarah Chapman, her 36-year-old slightly frail, and very pregnant daughter, rhythmically turned the crank on the steel apple peeler, creating a nearly endless spiral chain of peels. Wilma Spellman, Maggie's daughter-in-law, mixed the contents of a large porcelain bowl, pausing occasionally to stir the contents of one, or both of the copper kettles. Even Emy helped, sprinkling flour over the rolled crusts, at Maggie's direction. In fact, Emy was good at sprinkling flour. She got it all over the crust, the wooden countertop, herself, her Grandma, and a good portion of the floor. Jacob and Joseph Chapman, 4-year-old twins, loved it when Emy got flour on the floor. They loved to run through the kitchen and see their footprints follow them across the hard wood floors, into the dining room.

"Jacob, Joseph, stay out of the kitchen," Wilma called after the giggling little boys.

"It's alright Wilma" Maggie said with a tired smile. "Leave the boys be. I'll clean up later."

"I don't want them to wake up Grandpa." Wilma replied.

Maggie stopped rolling the crust. She let go of the rolling pin, wiped her hands on her apron, and brushed away a tear, smudging flour on her cheek.

"I'm sorry Momma," Wilma said. "I didn't mean to... "

"Don't be sorry," Maggie sniffled, waving away the apology.

Wilma and Sarah both stepped through the flour to give Maggie a hug.

"Are you alright Mom?" Sarah asked with a worried look.

"I'm fine." Maggie brushed her hair back with the back of her hand, flouring her graying hair just a bit grayer. "What about you? You look like you could use a break. Here, sit down." Maggie guided her pregnant daughter to a wooden stool, next to the counter.

"Is Grandpa going to be alright?" Emy asked.

"What did Doc Jones say?" Wilma asked, removing one of the copper kettles from the stove and pouring the contents into a large porcelain bowl.

Maggie sat down on a stool next to Sarah and sighed.

Wilma picked up a potato masher. "Emy, go keep an eye on your cousins, please," Wilma ordered, as she mashed the contents of the bowl.

"But Momma," Emy whined.

"Go! This here's girl talk."

"I'm a girl," Emy pleaded.

"And right now, you're a girl that needs to look after her cousins."

"Yes Momma." Emy clapped her hands together, creating a cloud of flour and sulked out of the kitchen.

"When you come back, I want you to sweep up this flour."

"Yes Momma." Emy's voice trailed away, as the flour cloud settled to the floor.

Wilma mashed the apples into sauce. Sarah, sitting on the stool, continued to peel the apples. Maggie, looking more tired than usual, placed her rolled pie crust into a clean pie plate and began to shape the edges.

"Tell us what Doc Jones had to say," Sarah pressed.

"Well, he's not right sure," Maggie said.

"Not sure. What do you mean he's not sure?" Sarah flared up.

"Doc said it could be any number of things."

"Such as?" Wilma asked.

"Such as... stroke. Or senility."

"Senile. Dad's not senile. A little crazy maybe, but certainly not senile," Sarah argued.

"You mean Alzheimer's?" Wilma questioned.

"Doc said Alzheimer's is pretty hard to detect, without tests," Maggie offered.

"What about a stroke?" Wilma asked.

"Doc said it could be. But, he shows no symptoms."

"Well if it isn't a stroke, and we know he's not senile, then what else could it be?" Sarah searched.

"Doc had one more possibility," Maggie offered hesitantly.

"What?" Sarah demanded.

Maggie's face clouded.

"What is it Mom?" Sarah said, a little softer.

Maggie looked up at her daughters. "P.D.S."

P.D.S. What's that?" Sarah and Wilma spoke at the same time.

"Doc called it Personality Displacement Syndrome. He said it's rare. But he's heard of it happening before. He's never seen it himself though."

"But what is... Personality Displacement Syndrome?" Wilma queried.

"Doc says that sometimes, after some traumatic event, a blow to the head, whatever, a patient can substitute their own personality, for someone else," Maggie tried to explain.

"Someone else! Why would Dad want to do that?" Sarah sputtered.

"I don't think he wants to do it. Doc says, it just happens," Maggie replied.

"P.D.S. I think I've heard of that before," Wilma said. "It's a psychological disorder."

"Psychological disorder. You're not saying Dad's gone crazy are you?" Sarah was getting angrier.

"Calm down Sweetheart," Maggie soothed. "Nobody's saying your Dad has gone crazy."

"Then what are you all saying?"

"Doc says Grandpa has a head injury. He's not sure what it is. Apparently, Dad believes he's from Seattle. He thinks he worked at the Seattle Times. Doc said Grandpa says he was on his way home from his last day of work when he fell," Maggie explained.

"Seattle?" Wilma questioned.

"What about us... his family?" Sarah was near to tears.

"I don't know. Doc doesn't think he thinks he has a family," Maggie explained.

All three women fell silent.

Buzzzzzzzzzzzzz.

The timer on the oven broke the heavy silence, and the three women jumped.

"Pies are done," Wilma said.

"Already! What time is it?" Maggie asked.

"Almost noon," Wilma said, as she picked up two hot pads and opened the oven. Hot air rushed out, stinging her face. She reached in quickly, and extracted a large apple pie, golden brown crust criss-crossing its top. She repeated her action with the second pie.

"I better get some lunch made for the little ones," Sarah said.

"We better stop yakin' and get something done," Maggie said, climbing off her stool.

"Mom?" Wilma placed her hand on Maggie's arm. "What should we do?"

"Yeah. What do we do about Grandpa? What do we tell the kids?" Sarah repeated.

"Give it time. Doc said to just give it some time. He's pretty sure his memory'll come back... eventually."

Maggie reset the timer on the oven and carefully placed two more pies inside.

CHAPTER SIX

ELI SWUNG HIS LEGS over the side of the bed and sat up. His head still hurt. He felt like Hell. His mouth tasted foul. "I haven't had a hang over like this since I got out of the Navy," Eli thought. He looked around the room. Same room. His watch was still sitting on the nightstand next to the bed. He picked it up and looked at it. He tried to open it. The latch looked broken. He pried open the cover. The crystal face was cracked. The hands were stopped at 6:25. "When I fell," he thought. He pushed closed the cover and put the watch in his Levi's pocket. He picked up the boots next to the bed and put them on. As he did, he noticed the 5 by 7 picture frame on the nightstand next to where his watch had been. He picked up the frame and examined the black and white picture. A family picture. He was in the picture. The woman he knew as Maggie was standing next to him. The little girl, Emy, was there. Twelve more people were in the photo, six adults and six children. A big group. They all looked happy, including him. But it couldn't be him. It must be somebody that looks like him. This must all be a terrible mistake. They think I'm somebody else.

He stood up and realized he hadn't gone to the bathroom in a very long time. He stepped across the room to the master bath, flipped the light switch, raised the seat, unzipped his pants and relieved himself. Aaaah. Blessed relief.

He lowered the seat. Turned on the faucet. Picked up the hand soap and washed his hands. He bent down, took a drink directly from the faucet, then splashed his face with water. He reached for the hand towel next to the tile countertop and dried his face, then his hands. He looked in the mirror above the sink. His was the face in the picture. His face. A little thin maybe, with a three-day growth, but, his face still the same. Who was it really? He had no memory of this place, or these people.

He stepped into the bedroom and looked around. It really was a nice bedroom. A ranch style bedroom. Not too fancy. Practical, in a friendly sort of way. The kind of bedroom he might like, if he ever had a house; nightstand on both sides of the bed, carved wooden headboard, six drawer dresser with a large mirror, a walk-in closet; and hardwood floors covered with a hand woven carpet.

It was the pictures that bothered him. Above the bed was a large portrait, a wedding portrait. As he stared at it, chills danced up and down his spine.

"She must be the prettiest girl I've ever seen."

Dressed in white, a slender, vibrant young Maggie looked deeply into the eyes of a tall, handsome young man, Eli thought looked remarkably like himself.

"They make a handsome couple."

It must be nice, to have someone, Eli thought. Maybe. Maybe it is me. Maybe, time really does 'unfold' us.

His hand found the security of the damaged watch, deep in his pocket. The spell was broken. What was he thinking? Years of loneliness and longing had buried him; buried him deep beneath the scrap-paper heaps of the Seattle Times refuse bins. He was alone. He had been alone. This was not his life. It was a case of mistaken identity, and he was going to get to the bottom of it. He turned away from the haunting portrait and carefully opened the bedroom door. The aroma of apple cinnamon pulled him into the hallway. His stomach growled. He was hungry. Very hungry.

* * *

Eli peered around the hallway corner, into the kitchen. Everything was quiet. "No one's home," he thought. Four delicious looking apple pies rested, tantalizingly, on the kitchen counter. Two dozen mason jars filled with apple sauce were stacked near the stove. A cookie sheet with apple tarts, dripping with frosting, sat on top of the stove. "Maybe I've died and gone to Heaven." Eli tiptoed into the kitchen, over to the stove. He picked up a tart and took a bite. "Ummmmmmmmmm." Apple filling, cinnamon, sugar frosting, still warm, melting. "I am in Heaven." He took another bite, bigger. And another. "Ohhhhhhh. This is good."

He looked around for something to drink. Nothing. He turned on the faucet and slurped a drink. "You'd think that when a body dies, they'd give him some kind of orientation, or something. Let 'em know who he was gonna spend eternity with. Like the Times. They was good at orientation. Everybody in their place. Doing their meaningless jobs. Combine all those meaningless jobs and you get a life-time of paper scraps." Eli bit into another tart. "I guess I shouldn't be so hard on the Times. I did get my gold watch." He felt the watch in his pocket. "Time to move on."

Eli picked up two more apple tarts and quietly stepped out of the kitchen. He walked down a short hallway, toward the back of the house. He opened the back door and stepped into an enclosed porch. Voices. He froze. Voices. From the distance. He looked through the porch screen and could see some people picking apples in a thick orchard. He could hear children's voices laughing. Women's voices correcting. Men's voices directing. The outdoor sounds had a definite rhythm, not unpleasant.

Eli slowly pulled open the porch-screen door. Creeeeeak! "Somebody needs to fix that creak." Eli slipped out the screen door and dashed around the side of the house, crouching behind a large azalea bush. "I don't think they saw me." Breathing hard, he made another dash around to the front of the house, this time hiding behind a rhododendron bush. From behind the bush, he could see the gravel walk, leading up to the front of the house. The walk extended twenty yards to a dirt driveway. The dirt driveway began at an old barn and traveled out to a larger dirt road, passing through a wooden gate. A wooden sign, he couldn't read from where he crouched, hung over the gateposts. A large old willow tree stood between Eli and the walk. Beyond the willow, a large blue spruce shaded the house from the afternoon sun. A wooden rail fence enclosed the property and gave boundary to a pleasant green lawn. Cherry Trees lined the fence, on this side of the property. "Could be Heaven," Eli thought, not for the last time.

Eli sprang from his hiding place and ran into the willow covering.

"Grandpa!" Emy exclaimed.

Eli stopped dead in his tracks. "Shsssssh!" He held his finger to his lips. Emy was having a 'tea party' with her cousins, Chloe and Mary.

"Hide-n-seek?" Emy whispered. "Can we play?"

Eli had to think fast.

"That's right. Hide-n-seek," Eli whispered back.

"Oh boy," the girls exclaimed.

"Shsssh! You have to be quiet to play this game."

"Can I be it?" Emy exclaimed.

"Can I?" Mary said.

"Can I?" Chloe said.

"No!" Eli replied, gruffly. The girls were startled. "I'll be it."

"Yea!" they replied together.

"You run and hide, and I'll count to one hundred. Don't make a sound, or I'll be able to find you. Ready?"

"Ready!"

"Okay. Go!"

All three girls jumped up and ran out from under the cover of the willow. Eli began to count.

"One. Two. Three. Four. Five."

Eli looked out from under the willow.

"Six. Seven. Eight.

He ran from the cover of the willow, toward the road.

"Nine. Ten. Eleven."

He stopped behind a fruit tree at the edge of the yard.

"Twelve," breathe.

"Thirteen," breathe.

"Fourteen," breathe.

Eli took a last look at the house. The wooden sign above the gate caught his eye. Spellman Farms. He dashed across the dirt road, into the cover of another orchard.

"Grandpa?" The little girls' voices followed him on the breeze.

"Damn."

"Grandpa, where are you?"

Under the cover of the apple trees, Eli set off at a brisk walk, away from the house. "I'm not your Grandpa," he said out loud.

CHAPTER SEVEN

ELI HAD BEEN WALKING FOR what seemed like a long time, up and down gently rolling hills. Since his watch didn't work, he couldn't be sure how long. The sun was getting low and the tree shadows were getting long. He stayed off the dirt road, among the apple trees. An old model car—he didn't recognize what kind—passed by, slowly. He hid among the trees. "They're looking for me," he thought. The car drove on.

"So now what?" The two apple tarts were long gone. No food. No water. No idea where he was. He looked around. "I guess I could live on apples." The orchard seemed to stretch on forever. "This road must go somewhere." He kept walking.

The dirt road he was following met a paved road, and continued on. Eli stopped at the cross. Which way? A car crested the hill a quarter mile away. He hurried deeper into the orchard. The car passed in a flourish, headlights brightening the lowering dusk. Eli turned right. A road sign caught his eye. He rushed to meet it. "Salem, 12 miles," he read out loud. Salem? Massachusetts? Oregon? Twelve miles. "Where am I?" Eli was suddenly very tired. He trudged on.

When the sun went down, the temperature dropped. There was a definite fall bite to the air. Eli shivered. He looked up at the darkening night sky. Stars. More stars. The sky was amazing. "Someone must have flipped on the 'star switch,'" Eli thought. He looked for the Big Dipper. Following the handle, down to the cup, and up, to the North Star. The sky was bright, brighter than he had ever seen. "At least some things don't change." He shivered again, involuntarily, and quickened his pace.

He'd been walking long enough now, that any liquid the Big Dipper held would have drained out. Boy was he thirsty. And cold. And tired. He had taken to walking on the road. It was easier in the dark. He could see the rocks and bumps and avoid stumbling. He figured that he could cover about two-and-a-half miles an hour. So, guessing, he figured he had about another hour to get to Salem. Where ever that was. Maybe he could find out, in Salem.

As he walked down a steep hill, he came to a hollow with a small stream running through it. An old cement bridge, probably built during FDR's relief program, narrowed to one lane at the crossing. The sound of the stream was music. Eli left the road and ran down the steep incline to the streambed. He knelt beside the shallow brook and cupped the water to his mouth. Slurping. He couldn't get enough. He put his face in the water and sucked the cold liquid till he gasped for air. He did it again. Gasping. The water ran down his face and neck. His shirt was soaked. He plunged his face in again, and drank. He thought, "this must be the sweetest water I've ever tasted." Quenched.

He leaned back from the stream and felt the cold dampness bleed into his shirt. Now he was really cold. His body began to shake. Unsteadily, Eli stood up. Tired. Shaking. A sound. Car. Eli splashed through the shallow stream, to the other side. He scrambled up the steep bank, pulling briars, small trees for purchase. He hurried, desperately.

"Help!", he called out.

The sound grew closer. Eli crested the bank and rushed onto the one lane bridge. Headlights blinded him as he called out.

"Help me, please!" Eli screamed, waving his arms and shielding his eyes. The dragon glare brightened and roared, filling his eyes and ears. Eli jumped from its path and tumbled back down the bank. The dragon roared past.

In the stillness of the night, Eli could feel his heart. His own rhythm beat cadence for the stream. The wind played counterpoint as the leaves swayed, then rested, swayed then rested. Sleep. Cold. My watch!

Eli opened his eyes. Instinctively, he reached into his pocket for the security of his watch. "Got to move on."

He stood up, shaking against the cold. He climbed. Step, step, step. "Keep your feet moving." One foot after another, slowly, methodically, mechanically.

Triumph. He crested the bank and reached the cement bridge. Leaning against the stone guardrail he thought, "I hope I don't have to do that again." A breath of wind chilled his effort-warmed body and the shaking began again. Eli looked around. How much farther? "Where am I?"

A light twinkled through the apple trees. "A house."

Eli hurried toward the light, energized by the sign of life. He turned up a dirt drive similar to the one he left, hours ago. The welcoming light shone from the windows of a rambling farmhouse. Eli stumbled up the porch steps and rapped on the door, bone cold fingers aching with each blow. He heard footsteps inside. A gray haired woman in a flannel robe opened the door.

"Help me, please!" Eli almost shouted.

The woman recoiled, and backed up.

Eli pressed forward, placing his foot in the door.

"Please, I need help."

"Elijah?" The woman stared at him, recognition replacing fear. "For heavens sake, what happened." She threw open the door. "Come in. Come in." The woman pulled Eli through her open door. "Ben! Ben, come quick. Elijah's here," she called out.

"What's that Ruth?" Ben called out from the other room.

"Elijah's here," she called again, brushing the leaves from Eli's clothes. "You're soaking wet. Let me get you a blanket. You look like you're freezing."

A man in flannel pajamas about Eli's age shuffled into the room as Ruth opened a linen closet and pulled out a Pendleton wool blanket.

"Elijah? What in the sam-hill are you doin' here this time of night?" Ben said.

Ruth wrapped the blanket around Eli's shoulders.

"Could I use your phone?"

"Phone? What's wrong?" Ben asked.

"Are you hurt?," Ruth said.

"Has there been an accident?" Ben questioned.

"No! I'm fine." Eli's terminal reply cut them off.

Ruth and Ben stopped short. Eli shivered like a wet puppy. The silence was hardening. Ruth broke it.

"Eli, you're shivering. Let's get you out of those wet clothes. Ben, get Eli some of your clothes. The bathroom's right over there. Then you can tell us what happened." Ruth nearly pushed Eli into the bathroom.

When Eli came out of the bathroom with Ben's tight fitting clothes on—Eli was two sizes bigger than Ben—Ruth guided him into their small kitchen. Ben followed. Ben and Eli sat down at the kitchen table.

"What happened Eli? You look like you been through the war." Ben asked.

"You must be starving," Ruth said. "Let me fix you something." She began pulling items out of the cupboard.

"How do you know my name?", Eli asked.

Ruth and Ben looked at each, awkwardly.

"How do you know who I am?" Eli demanded, again.

"We heard about your fall," Ben said. "You feeling better?"

"How awful," Ruth didn't give Eli opportunity to answer. "You scared your family half to death. Maggie told me. I'm telling Ben all the time, you old men need to stay off those ladders. Leave it to the young men."

"Now Ruth, you'd best hold your tongue."

"I'll say what needs to be said, thank you very much."

Ben looked at Eli and smiled. "Women," he said.

"Humph!" Ruth winked at Eli and placed a turkey sandwich and a glass of milk before him.

He looked at them, and then looked at the sandwich. He really was hungry. He could find out who they were after he ate. He tore into the sandwich. "Ummmm," he felt. Things seem to taste better here.

"So what happened Eli?" Ben asked.

Eli swallowed a bite. "I'm just trying to get home."

"Home! I'll take you home," Ben said.

"I don't want to go home."

Ruth caught Ben's eye.

Ben looked at Eli. "What are you saying Eli?"

Eli took a long drink of milk, set the glass down and looked at his hands.

"I don't know who I am," he sighed. "I don't know who you are."

Ruth looked at Ben.

"I have no memory of this place," Eli whispered.

Ruth sat down next to Ben and put her hand on his shoulder.

"Can you help me?" Eli pleaded.

Ben exhaled. "Of course Elijah. Of course we'll help you. What do you want us to do?"

"Where am I?" Eli asked.

"This here's our farm," Ben said, concerned.

"No Ben. He means where do we live. Right Eli?" Ruth said.

Eli nodded.

"Well, like I said, this here's our farm. It's about 8 miles from your... from Spellman Farms. We're just about 4 miles outside Salem."

"Salem, Oregon?" Eli questioned.

Ben looked at Ruth and smiled. "No," he said. "Salem, Washington. Salem, Oregon's the big city."

"Salem, Washington! Never heard of it. How-n-the-hell did I get here?" Eli exclaimed.

Ruth's cheeks colored.

"Settle down Eli. Why don't you tell us what you do remember. Then, maybe we can help," Ben said.

Eli took a deep breath. "I'm sorry. It's just that things... I don't under-stand... "

"It's alright," Ruth said. "Go ahead Eli, tell us what you remember."

Eli took a deep breath and began. He told them an unexpected story, his story, a story of loneliness and pain. When he finally ran out of words, he took the gold watch from his pocket and placed it gently on the table, as proof. Ruth, Ben and Eli stared at the watch in silence. Ben reached out and picked up the watch, surveying it carefully.

"That's the damnedest thing I've ever heard," Ben said.

"Ben, don't say such things," Ruth replied.

"Well it is," Ben said. "I don't know what to make of it. I've known Eli for 25 years."

Eli slammed his hand down on the table.

"Then how come I don't know you," he shouted.

"I don't know Eli. I truly don't know," Ben whispered, putting the watch back down.

Eli stood up.

"I'd better go," he said.

Ben and Ruth stood up too.

"We'll take you home,' Ruth said. "Your family must be worried sick."

"Home?" Eli said.

"That's right. Home," Ruth stated matter-of-factly. "And, we'll tell you all about it on the way."

* * *

The old truck turned onto the dirt drive and proceeded down the lane. Ben drove. Ruth sat in the middle. Eli leaned against the door.

"Spellman Farms," Ruth read, as the truck headlights passed under the overhanging sign.

"The man can read," Ben said.

"Don't you think I know that?" Ruth shot back. "I'm just filling in the details he don't remember. That's all."

"Enough with the details. The man's got to figure this out on his own," Ben said.

The truck pulled up to the farmhouse and stopped. Eli stared out the window, but didn't move. A light shone through the kitchen window.

Ruth put her hand on Eli's shoulder.

"It'll be alright Elijah," she said.

He didn't move.

The kitchen door flew open and Maggie Spellman ran out, across the porch and down the steps into the drive. She stopped short, her hands covering her mouth, as if she were praying. The night breeze rustled the folds of her cotton robe.

"She sure is pretty," Eli thought.

"This is your home," Ruth said.

Eli opened the truck door and stepped out. He stood by the truck and looked at Maggie. Their eyes met. She took a step towards him. Slowly, Eli took a step towards her. Maggie's pace quickened, then stopped, standing very still, vulnerable, before him. She looked up at Eli. The moonlight danced across her hair. Eli raised his heavy arms and found them lightened by Maggie's body, as he held her, for the first time he could remember. Over Eli's shoulder, Maggie mouthed the words, "thank you."

Ruth wiped a glistening tear-drop from her eye as Maggie buried her head in Eli's shoulder.

"Take me home Ben."

Without a word, Ben coaxed the old truck into gear.

Eli looked back, only for a moment, then, with his arm around Maggie, the couple walked quietly back to the farmhouse.

CHAPTER EIGHT

THE NIGHT SKY WAS BRILLIANT. The stars were so bright Eli barely needed headlights. He held the wheel of his aging Ford Falcon with one hand and with his other, he held the hand of his new bride, Mrs. Elijah Spellman—Maggie. "Love Me Tender" played on the radio. Maggie snuggled closer to Eli and rested her head on his shoulder. Eli could hardly believe it. Maggie Hamilton was his.

Eli and Maggie met at Seattle Pacific University, just after Eli got out of the Navy. Eli was studying to be an Engineer. Maggie worked as a secretary to one of his professors. From the beginning, she was the apple of his eye. The plan was to spend their 5 day honeymoon driving the North Cascade Highway. Eli had rented a cabin near Lake Chelan for two glorious days. Now they were headed back through the Yakima Valley for the fall harvest festival. They hoped to stay the night at a little cottage near Cle Elum, but had gotten lost somewhere after Enumclaw. Strange Indian names. Eli could never quite get used to them. Anyway, it didn't matter. Eli felt like he could drive forever—his girl by his side—a starry night. It didn't get any better than this.

The aging Falcon seemed to hum down the narrow country road. "Earth Angel" followed "Love Me Tender". Maggie sighed contentedly. Eli smiled. The Falcon crested a small hill and the headlights gleamed off an old road-sign.

ONE LANE BRIDGE.

Eli touched the brake lightly. No traffic on this road.

Suddenly, Eli saw an old man stagger onto the bridge. The Falcon continued to travel at full speed. But, for Eli, time changed. He seemed to see things from outside himself. The old man waved and screamed. Eli slammed on the brakes. There was no where for him to go. He couldn't stop in time. He was going to run over this mad man.

Maggie Screamed.

Eli turned the wheel hard.

The tires screeched.

The man disappeared.

The car crashed into the stone guardrail. Bounced. Spun. Crashed into the other guardrail. Spun again. The front windshield exploded. Maggie disappeared.

Eli stood by the stone guardrail of the one-lane bridge. The mangled Ford Falcon steamed from the bottom of the gully below. Eli watched as a young man, bleeding from the nose and forehead kicked his way out of the car, and fell into the mud bank. The man was frantic. He screamed!

"Maggie."

He splashed into the stream, waste deep.

"Maggie."

He reached for something. Limp.

"Oh God. NO!"

Desperation.

Watching from the bridge, Eli began to sob.

The man screamed. "Help me!" He looked right at Eli, pleading.

Eli screamed, "Maggie." The man screamed, "Maggie."

Eli scrambled down the bank, falling into the mud. He fell into the water. The car hissed at him.

"Maggie. Oh, Maggie."

He pulled at the woman's body. He saw her face beneath the water, white, vacant.

"No. No."

Desperately, he pulled at her. He fell in, flailing.

"Maggie. Maggie. Maggie."

"Eli."

She spoke.

Desperately, he fought to free her.

"Eli." Her hand reached his, fingertips touching.

"Maggie."

"Eli, wake up!"

Eli sat up in the big double bed. "Maggie." His arms were flailing and his wild eyes looked beyond the room.

"Eli wake up. It's alright. I'm right here."

Maggie tried to hold onto him as he thrashed about the bed.

"Maggie?"

"I'm right here. It's alright. You were dreaming."

"Maggie." Eli, reached out for her as violent sobs wrenched his frame.

Maggie pulled him close, comforting.

"It's alright, honey. I'm right here."

"The car. The crash."

"It's alright. It was only a dream."

"You were thrown through the windshield."

"I'm right here."

"The man on the bridge. I tried to swerve."

"It was just a dream."

"But it seemed so real." Eli sobbed, and shook.

"Calm down Sweetheart. It's just a dream."

"You drowned. I saw you." His sobs began to slow.

Maggie wiped his perspiration drenched face and neck with her robe.

"I'm here Eli. Right here with you."

"Thank God." Eli pulled her close to him, and shook. His sobs subsiding.

Maggie stroked Eli's gray hair, until his breathing slowed, and he loosened his hold. Eli swung his legs over the edge of the bed and switched on the light.

Maggie followed suit. They both sat quietly on the edge of the bed for some moments. Eli stared into the distance. He shivered.

"Let me fix us a cup of hot cocoa while you put on some dry pajamas," Maggie said.

Eli slowly turned and looked into Maggie's eyes.

"It was so real," he whispered.

She took his hand and pressed it to her check.

"This is real," she said.

He caressed her skin. "It can't be."

She looked deep in his eyes. He could see his reflection. He stood up suddenly, pulling her with him.

"Cocoa sounds good," he said. And he stepped into the bathroom and closed the door.

CHAPTER NINE

MAGGIE FLIPPED THE KITCHEN LIGHT SWITCH, and squinted hard, deepening the furrows beneath her eyes. She filled a copper kettle with water and set it on the stove to heat. The grandfather clock in the living room sang four tones, 4:15 a.m., the darkest part of the night. Lately, she had been seeing a lot of the darkness, not much light. Since Eli's fall, she felt like she had been living in a dream, a bad dream. Just what was going on in his mind, she couldn't begin to imagine. How could someone you had known your whole life suddenly change? Who was he? Was this a sign of mental illness? Alzheimer's?

Maggie padded through the kitchen and into the living room. She reached down and pulled a scrapbook off the bottom shelf and padded back into the kitchen. Memories. She flipped open the scrapbook.

Steam was rising from the kettle, so she pulled two mugs from the kitchen cabinet and placed them on the table. She took a spoon from the drawer, went to the pantry and grabbed two packages of Swiss Miss Instant Cocoa. She set them by the mugs. Memories. She looked at the scrapbook.

Last summer, Sarah had convinced her to take a scrapbooking class. At first, she had felt overwhelmed, trying to organize a lifetime of memories in one little book. Sarah had to continually remind her that you do it, one page at a time. Surprisingly, she found she really enjoyed it. That was about a dozen scrapbooks ago. Now, she had ideas for organizing. She bought special acid free paper. She had die-cuts and stickers and press-on type, and she even went to weekend seminars. She smiled as she looked at the first page of 'Highlights, 1968'. That was the summer Sarah was born. Maggie grimaced, longingly, at a picture of herself, 8 months pregnant. She was swollen, and huge. Tommy and Andy stood on each side of her, pretending that her stomach was a basket-ball.

Maggie turned the page. Eli, wearing scrubs, held tiny Sarah, ten days old, in ICU at County Hospital. Maggie's breath caught, even now, thinking about how they nearly lost her. Frail Sarah struggled most of her life with one health problem or another. She hasn't had an easy time with this pregnancy either. "I guess that's what Grandma's do—worry," Maggie thought.

"What are you worried about?"

Maggie jumped.

"I didn't see you come into the kitchen," she said.

"From the looks of these pictures, I've been here for awhile," Eli said.

Maggie smiled.

"Ready for some cocoa?"

Eli smiled back.

Maggie took the kettle from the stove and poured the steaming liquid into the mugs. Tearing the Swiss Miss packets, she poured the chocolate in and stirred, spoon tinkling on porcelain. She went to the fridge and took out a can of ready-mix whipped cream and slurped it in.

"Just the way you like it," Maggie said, handing the steaming chocolate to Eli.

He took a drink and sighed his satisfaction. Maggie sat on the stool next to him. Neither one spoke. Maggie turned a scrapbook page.

"Remember this one Honey?" Maggie said. She laughed at a photo of her and Eli at the Fall Harvest. Eli was wearing farmer overalls and holding a pitchfork. Maggie was wearing a jumper and holding an apple pie. The Farmer and his wife.

"Did I really dress like that?" Eli questioned.

"You! Just look at my dress."

"What's wrong with your dress?"

Maggie sighed and turned the page. Eli sipped his cocoa.

"Remember our trip to Seattle that year?" Maggie said wistfully.

"No!" Eli stated.

Maggie looked up, warily.

"What?" she asked.

Eli stood up.

"No," he said. "I don't remember our trip to Seattle."

Maggie stood up and put her hand on Eli's arm.

"Oh Honey, I'm sorry. I didn't mean to..."

"I said, I don't remember our trip to Seattle. I didn't say I don't remember."

Maggie took her hand from Eli's arm and touched the scrapbook.

"Eli, this is our life. These are our memories."

"They're not mine!"

"Look Eli. Look at these pictures. You're in nearly everyone of them—because I'm always the one taking the pictures."

She folded the page, covering up her picture.

"It's me you'll have trouble finding in here, not you."

"THAT'S NOT ME." Eli turned away.

Maggie began to cry, softly. Eli turned around.

"Look...I'm sorry. I don't remember. It looks like me. But it can't be me. How can it be me?"

"I don't know Eli. Doc says it'll all come back to you."

Eli grabbed her with both hands.

"Don't you understand? It's not that I don't remember. I remember just fine. But I remember something else. Not this."

Maggie began sobbing in earnest.

"What Eli? What?"

He released his hold on her and ripped a page from the scrapbook, holding it up.

"Not this!"

"Then what Eli? Tell me what memories you have that could be any better than what we have had together."

"I'm not making this up."

"Your family needs you."

He put the scrapbook page down on the counter.

"I don't have a family."

She picked up the page and held it.

"You do now."

He turned away.

"What are you going to do?" she asked.

"I'm going to Seattle."

"The Harvest Festival's coming up. The boys'll need your help with the cider booth."

"I've got to find out."

Maggie stood up and put her arm on Eli's shoulder, attempting to turn him.

"I'm going with you," she said.

"Suit yourself."

Without looking at her, Eli walked away.

CHAPTER TEN

THEY LEFT THE NEXT AFTERNOON. It took them both that long to recover from the sleepless night. Eli drove their twenty-year-old Pontiac. Tom and Andy, their middle son, had both tried to talk Eli out of going. Sarah called Doc, but they left before he could arrive. Eli felt like he had to get out of there before he drowned. He wanted to go alone, but couldn't make himself tell Maggie not to come along. Besides, if he went alone, he wasn't sure he'd come back. And he wasn't ready to admit he didn't want to leave.

So they drove into Salem along the same road Eli had walked. The one-lane bridge looked a lot different in the daylight—smaller, and less frightening. Even so, Eli shivered as he drove over it.

Salem was nothing like he expected. It was small. One main street— small. One gas station—small. But there was a square, home to the famous Harvest Festival he kept hearing about. So, he figured, that must make it a town. And Eli drove through it, seeing it for the first time. Someone waved. Maggie waved back.

"Sharon Swenson," she said.

"Oh," he said, turning onto the main road heading towards Yakima.

In Yakima they picked up highway 82 North, into Ellensburg.

"We haven't been this way in years," Maggie said, hopefully.

"Hmmph," Eli grunted. He didn't want to talk about it.

In Ellensburg, they picked up I-90, traveling through the Cascade Mountains toward Seattle. Steel gray clouds haunted the craggy peaks, just below the snow level, while the evergreen clad mountains turned black beneath the ghostly wisps.

"Aren't these mountains magnificent," Maggie said.

"I hadn't noticed," Eli said.

But as they drove, memories flooded Eli's mind. The last time he drove over Snoqualmie pass was on their honeymoon. He thought she died. He looked over at Maggie. She smiled. Eli began to sweat. His knuckles turned white, squeezing the wheel. The color drained from his face.

"Are you alright Sweetheart?" Maggie asked.

They crested the pass. Eli death-gripped the wheel. The aging Pontiac began to wail a reckless song down the steep mountain grade. Maggie set her knitting down on the seat between them. Eli stared straight ahead, foot pressed firmly into the floor.

"Eli, what's the matter." Maggie instinctively pressed both feet against the brake she couldn't find. The tires moaned as the Pontiac fought against a curve, much faster than the yellow road sign recommended. Beads of sweat broke over Eli's forehead, cascading down his cheeks. His knuckles matched the rugged snowcapped peaks.

"Eli, slow down. Please," Maggie said.

No response.

Eli was breathing hard. Out of control. He shot past a logging truck in the slow lane, into a cloud, sitting heavy on the mountain slope. The world turned gray. He leaned forward, peering into the fog. The mountain slope called the old Pontiac. Faster. Faster.

Maggie reached over and touched Eli. Eli looked at her. The cloud lifted. Maggie screamed. Blunt ends of a trailer filled with Douglas fir seemed to be racing right at them. Eli felt the brake surrender. The car began to slide on the specter slickened highway. Memories began to slide before his eyes like paper on a press. "Maggie." His own voice seemed to blend with the distant roar of the press. Maggie pressed her hands against the dashboard. The Pontiac shook with a will of its own. Rubber tires found purchase. Douglas fir screeched away, instead of toward. Eli pumped the brake and pulled off the highway. The gravel shoulder pinged against the undercarriage as the old Pontiac crunched to a stop. Acrid rubber smoke wafted past the old car. Eli held fast to the steering wheel, breathing hard. Maggie stared straight ahead, weeping softly. Eli turned the key. Silence.

The Pontiac began to creak and tick as the outside coolness invaded the car. Eli turned slowly and stared at Maggie.

"I'm sorry," he said.

No response.

A logging truck streaked by, shaking the car and muddying the windshield.

"I'm sorry," he said again.

Maggie turned slowly and looked at Eli, tears cooling the heat of her cheeks.

" For as long as I have known you Eli, I have always felt safe. Until now." Maggie opened the car door, stepped out into the cool mountain drizzle and slammed the door. Eli could barely see her through the foggy windshield, as she began to walk down the highway. He slammed his fist into the steering wheel and jumped out of the car.

"Maggie," he called.

No response.

She just kept walking.

"Maggie, come back."

No response.

Eli began to walk.

"Maggie, where're you going?"

No response.

Eli quickened his pace.

"Come on Mag. It's starting to rain."

No response.

Eli began to jog.

"Maggie. Please." Eli caught her by the arm.

"Don't touch me," she said. She shook his arm away and continued walking. Her hair began to drip as the drizzle thickened. She wiped her forehead.

"I said I was sorry."

She stopped.

"You could have killed us both."

He stopped.

She turned and began to walk. He followed.

"Where do you think you're gonna go?" he said.

"North Bend," she said without turning around.

"North Bend? Are you crazy?" Eli said.

Maggie stopped and turned, hands on her hips.

"Am I crazy?" she said. Her look froze Eli. She began to walk. "I'll call Wilma. She can come and pick me up."

"Maggie please. I'm sorry," he said. She stopped again.

"Look Eli. I don't know who you are anymore. You've got this crazy idea that you're somebody else. Fine. Be somebody else. Live somebody else's life. Go find yourself. Just leave me out of it."

Rain mixed with tears on Maggie's face. Her hair matted against her forehead. Her knit sweater clung limply to her plump frame. She shivered against the cold.

"I didn't ask you to come with me," Eli said.

Maggie clenched her fists and nearly growled. She turned and stomped down the highway.

"Come on Maggie, get back in the car. You can't walk to North Bend. It's five miles down the road." Eli chased her. He tried to grab her. She shrugged off his arm.

"I said don't touch me." She kept walking

"Maggie, I've got to know. Don't you see? I don't know who I am?"

"If you weren't so damned old, I'd say you were having a mid-life crisis. Now, I just think you're crazy."

"Maggie, please. What if these memories are real? What if I'm not who you think I am?"

"Come on Eli. We've grown up together. I've lived with you for nearly fifty years. I know everything there is to know about you."

Now Eli stopped walking. He looked up through the fog, at the frosted mountain peaks and yelled.

"Who am I?"

The fog seemed to suck his voice into obscurity. No echo. He stood there. Looking up. Maggie watched him. He raised his fists.

"Why am I here?"

No response.

An eighteen-wheeler roared past. The mud and water hit him from behind. The draft pushed him forward. He took a stumble step. He hung his arms. He wiped his face. He turned around and walked toward the car.

"Eli!" Maggie called out.

He stopped, but didn't turn around. Maggie, pulled by his gravity, took two steps toward him.

"Eli, wait."

His shoulders slumped. He turned around. He was soaking wet.

"Do you want me with you?" Maggie called out.

Eli's lips moved. Another truck raced past, robbing Maggie of the answer. He stood there, by the side of the highway, twenty-five feet from her. She took two more steps. She'd known him all his life. But, she didn't know him now.

"Eli, please. Do you want me?"

His lips moved again.

"Yes." The word seemed to reach her ears with the drifting fog.

"Yes." It was enough.

She ran to him. She hugged him. The rain fell harder. Tears or raindrops. It was hard to tell.

CHAPTER ELEVEN

THE HEATER WAS RUNNING FULL BLAST. The windows kept fogging up. Eli took the North Bend exit off of I-90.

"What are you doing?" Maggie asked.

"We've got to dry out some. I figure we can spend the night here and drive home in the morning."

"What about Seattle?" she asked.

"Not going," he said.

Eli turned right off the highway. The sign said, 'Snoqualmie lodge'. It looked warm.

"What do you mean we're not going?" she said.

Exasperation. "Just what it sounds like," he said.

"Oh no you don't. You aren't gonna blame this on me. We don't come all this way and not see it through."

Eli pulled the car up to the mountain chalet. Headlights caught the trail sign, 'Snoqualmie Falls 1/4 mile'. He turned off the engine.

"O.K. what if we get there and find out that really is...was my life? Then what?"

Maggie laughed. "I'm not too worried."

Eli didn't laugh. "You should be."

He got out of the car. Maggie stopped laughing. He opened her door, and together they went inside the lodge.

"Good evening," the desk clerk said. He had on a red flannel cap, covering both ears. He was too young and skinny to be a lumberjack.

Maggie smiled. Eli nodded.

"What brings you out to our fine establishment on this rainy evening?" he said.

"We'd like a room," Eli said.

The lumberjack wannabe shook his head and smirked. The cap flapped against his ears. "I see," he said. "Is this your first time?"

"What?" Eli growled.

The clerk stammered, his face matching the color of his cap, "I mean, is this your first time staying with us?"

"Yes!" Eli barked.

The clerk began typing on the computer. "Name please?"

"Spellman," Eli said.

The clerk looked down his very long nose, "will that be one rooooom-mmm...or twoooo?"

"One!" Eli turned to Maggie, "what kind of a place is this anyway?"

She put her hand on his arm.

"Actually," she said, "this is our second time."

"Reeeeeeally," the clerk said, continuing to type.

"Yes," Maggie said. "My husband and I stayed here many years ago. Long before you were born. On our honeymoon."

"Ohhh. I see. Did you enjoy your stay?"

Maggie squeezed Eli's arm and rubbed his shoulder. "Verrry much. Do you think we could have that honeymoon suite again."

Eli scowled.

The clerk stopped typing and looked up at Maggie and Eli. "Dude, you're, like, my grandparents."

"Just give us a room please," Eli said.

Maggie mouthed the words, 'I'm just having some fun.'

"Card," the clerk said.

"What?" Eli said.

"Credit card," the clerk said, still typing.

"Oh," Eli said, pulling out his wallet. He took out a MasterCard and handed it to the clerk. The clerk swiped the card and began to type some more.

"Smoking or non," he said.

"Non," Maggie said.

"King, Queen, or two doubles," he said.

Maggie and Eli looked at each other. Their cheeks turned red.

"King," Eli said.

"Dude!" the clerk said smiling. He typed some more.

He kept typing.

He hit return. He typed some more.

"Are you doing homework, or getting us a room?" Eli growled.

The clerk hit return again. The dot matrix printer began to sing. A small piece of paper began to spew forth.

"Just put your ol' John Hancock right there, and you've got yourself a rooooom for the night."

Eli took the paper and signed his name.

"Oh, Dude, I almost forgot. The lodge has a special tonight in the restaurant. Dinner by the fireside. All you can eat fried chicken. Check it out. Here's you key...suite 411." He winked at Maggie.

"Thanks...dude," she said.

Eli picked up their suitcase and they walked toward their room.

* * *

The Maitre d' welcomed them into the rustic lodge dining room. He was wearing Levi's, a white button down shirt with a black bow-tie, and a Pendleton wool overshirt.

"Lumberjack, or busboy?" Eli whispered to Maggie.

"Could we have a table near the fire?" Maggie asked.

"Certainly," the Maitre d' said. "Right this way."

The Maitre d' seated them near the cavernous fireplace. A few massive logs crackled on the fire. The room held the slight scent of campfire, mixed with baking bread. Very inviting. He set the menus on the table.

"Tonight's specials are..."

"Fried chicken," Eli interrupted.

"Yes, that's right. And..."

"That's what we want," Eli said. "Fried chicken."

"Would you like something to drink?" The Maitre d' rushed to beat Eli.

"Water," Eli said.

"Very well," the Maitre d' said, removing the menus. "Sally will be right with you." And the Maitre d' lumbered away.

"Eli look," Maggie exclaimed.

An older man, dressed in traditional Bavarian costume stepped up to a raised platform and began to play the accordion.

"Isn't this wonderful," Maggie said.

"Everybody polka," Eli said.

"Come on Eli, enjoy yourself," Maggie said, just as Sally the waitress, dressed in a Bavarian milkmaid outfit arrived.

"OK, I will," Eli said in response to Sally's smile. Maggie scowled. Sally placed two empty glasses on the table and began to pour. She started low and raised the pitcher above her head, still pouring water in a cascade waterfall. Maggie leaned back, expecting her to spill. Full glass. She started again on Eli's glass. Low, stretching the stream to her full height. Eli's eyes grew big. Full glass.

"Wonderful," Maggie exclaimed.

"Thank you Ma'am," Sally said.

"Do you ever miss?" Eli asked.

"Sometimes." Sally winked at Maggie. Maggie laughed out loud. Sally placed some fresh baked steaming rolls on the table.

"Would you like some honey with your rolls?" Sally asked.

"Of course," Maggie said.

Sally placed a small dish on the table next to each dinner plate. She dipped a ladle into a honey jar and began to drip a thickening stream of honey onto the center of the plate, in the same manner she poured the water. She raised the ladle as high as she could while dripping the honey into the dish. She swirled the honey, cut off the stream, and began again on Eli's dish. Maggie laughed in delight. Eli looked skeptical.

"Would you like an appetizer, before dinner?" Sally asked.

"No, thank you," Eli said.

"Alrighty then, I'll be right back with your dinner," Sally said, as she pranced away.

"I hope she doesn't drop it on us," Eli said.

"Eli!" Maggie scolded.

"Well?" Eli said.

The fire crackled and popped. The accordion music, usually annoying, seemed, surprisingly happy. Maggie and Eli both dipped their hot rolls in the honey dishes and savored the warm, thick sweetness. Sally brought their steaming fried chicken, with mashed potatoes and gravy. Maggie held a leg with both hands. Eli tasted the breast. Juice dripped down his chin.

"Finger food," he said with a mouth full.

Maggie laughed.

They talked and they were warmed. They were filled. They were content.

Eli could not remember a dinner more pleasant. Maggie could not remember a time without Eli.

"I'm glad we stopped here," she said. "It's been a long time since we got away by ourselves."

"More water?" Sally asked, not waiting for a reply. She released the spillway, sending a stream cascading from above. Ice cold drops splashed on Eli's arms.

"Sorry," Sally smiled, and disappeared.

Eli wiped his arm with a napkin.

"I don't remember," he said. "I'm sorry."

Maggie leaned forward and put her hand on Eli's hand.

"I do," she said. "I remember, Eli. All of it."

Eli frowned and stared into the fire. Maggie squeezed his hand.

"Our whole life together Eli. It's been wonderful. Heart wrenching. Difficult. Joyful. I wouldn't trade one minute of it."

Eli turned and looked into Maggie's eyes. His reflection shimmered in the dancing firelight. Eli wanted to remember. He wanted to believe he had built a life with this woman. But he couldn't. He just couldn't remember. It couldn't be. His memories of being alone were too strong. But, he wanted to believe. He could see that she believed. Maybe he could believe in her. Maybe she could give him her memories.

"Excuse me! Do you have time for a little desert," Sally smiled hopefully.

The accordion player stopped abruptly. The small crowd clapped appreciatively. Maggie pulled her hand away and clapped. The spell was broken.

"Thank you! Thank you very much," the Bavarian Elvis said. He honked his accordion and pointed at Sally, "I'llllll be baaaack." Sally giggled.

"No thanks," Maggie said.

"Then here's your check," Sally said.

Eli reached in his pocket for his wallet. What he found was cold and hard. 'My watch,' he thought.

"What time is it Sweetheart?" Maggie said.

"Time to go," Eli groused. He stood up and pulled a twenty from his other pocket. He slapped it on the table and walked away. Maggie grabbed his hand as he strode by. She smiled a 'thank you' at Sally as Eli towed her from the room.

"Come again," Sally said, as they disappeared through the door.

* * *

Eli leaned back against two fluffy pillows on the far side of the king size bed. 'Nice room,' he thought. 'I can't believe I'm paying for it.'

Maggie opened the door and came out of the bathroom. Her soft cotton nightgown swirled around her soft round body. Eli stared at the blank television screen, pretending not to notice. Maggie switched off the light. Without a word, she slid across the bed and snuggled up against him. Moonlight danced through the parted window coverings and played in the highlights of her hair. Eli held very still. Maggie placed her hand on Eli's chest and felt the aging, yet still firm muscles. Her hand traced the contour of his chest. Eli held his breath. Maggie opened one button of his pajama top and put her hand inside, touching his skin. Warmth. Eli sucked in his breath. Maggie rubbed her hand across his chest. Heat. Eli flinched, and grabbed her hand. She looked up from his shoulder, trying to see his eyes in the pale moonlight. Eli stared straight ahead, frozen. Maggie pulled her hand away from his chest and sat up, trying to make eye contact.

"It's alright Eli," she said softly.

No response.

She touched his shoulder.

He slowly turned his head to look at her, as if from a great distance. Silhouette. Their eyes met.

Frightened.

"Please?" she whispered.

Trembling.

He put his hand on hers.

"I...can't," his lips barely moved.

"Oh Eli."

A tear. Silver stream. Snow melt. Cascade. Embrace.

They held each other close. Under covers. Restless dreams. Dreamless sleep.

CHAPTER TWELVE

THEY HAD A CONTINENTAL BREAKFAST in the lodge coffee shop and checked out by 8:30. Eli figured it would take them about an hour-and-a-half to get to his apartment. He wanted to start there first. He wanted to show Maggie what kind of life he had lived before…"before what," he thought. "She'll never understand. Hell. I don't understand."

Eli drove in silence. Maggie said nothing. They came out of the mountains, into the foothill community of Issaquah.

"Beautiful country," Eli said.

Maggie smiled and nodded, but did not speak. "Fine, don't say anything. I like it that way," Eli thought. He didn't want to admit that he'd gotten used to hearing her voice. Morning Song. The silence, which he would say he wanted was louder than he could bear. He switched on the radio.

"Drive time traffic on the ones," the announcer droned. "Expect delays on the 5 north, near University. There's an accident on the Mercer Island bridge, snarling traffic into the city from the East. And, if you expect to get through downtown Seattle this morning, you'd better have a triple latte. Traffic brought to you by Seattle's own Starbucks. Back to you, Uncle Joe. Thanks Sky Cap…"

Eli switched off the radio. Noise. Congestion. He was grateful he never owned a car. Well, present life excepted.

"How do people drive in traffic everyday?" he thought, out loud.

No response. They drove on.

A steady rain fell, as they crossed Lake Washington on the floating bridge. Traffic was slow, but not impossible. Eli found that he really wanted to go slow. He wasn't used to driving in traffic. As far as he could remember, he wasn't used to driving at all. But, somewhere inside him, he felt as congested as the traffic. He felt a heaviness in his chest.

"I'm surprised there aren't more accidents on this bridge," he said out loud.

Maggie watched the storm blow waves up against the railings.

"Is it really a floating bridge?" she asked.

"That's what they say," he replied.

The fog had thickened enough and the rain fell hard enough that they could barely tell when they'd crossed the Lake.

"I'm not sure which exit to take," Eli said. "I don't usually drive in the city."

"Where are we going?" Maggie asked.

"My apartment," Eli said. "I wonder what they've done with my things. Then, we'll go to the Times. I want to show you where I worked."

Eli was beginning to get excited. He looked across at Maggie. She looked away, staring out the passenger window. She didn't speak.

Eli drove into the city, with the crawling traffic. Nothing looked familiar. Of course, he never drove. I-90, I-5 junction 1 mile. Safeco Field 1.5 miles. Airport Way/Freeway End 2 miles.

"What do I do," Eli said, confused.

"Safeco Field," Maggie said. "I've always wanted to see the Mariners play."

"We're not here to see a baseball game," Eli barked.

"That's alright," Maggie mused. "The Mariners aren't any good this year anyway. I'm sure they didn't make the playoffs."

Eli took the exit. Atlantic Street. "Funny," he thought, "For the west coast." SAFECO FIELD, HOME OF THE SEATTLE MARINERS. The stadium loomed before them, surrounded by concrete pillars and overpasses. Train tracks fought for light beneath the mammoth monoliths of industrial construction. ALASKAN WAY VIADUCT/1ST AVENUE.

"First avenue," Eli said. "That's where I live."

The light turned red. Eli stopped. Maggie felt claustrophobic beneath the over, and over again passes. A homeless guy, shaggy beard and tattered clothes, leaned against a concrete pillar, trying to escape the rain. He shook his torn cardboard box sign at the world. 'Work for food.' The letters were smeared. The light turned red. Eli turned left. The onramp to the Alaskan Way viaduct rose from the dirty concrete floor of the city, and lifted them above the filth. The viaduct ran above the waterfront. Gray sky met charcoal water just beyond their reach. Gigantic cranes rose into the fog hoisting rusted containers from stained ships. The rain turned to drizzle. The viaduct gently descended and set them down on 1st Avenue, the industrial section.

"We're almost there," Eli said.

No response.

Eli slowed down as he drove past the fortress like gate of Todd Shipyards. He pulled into a small, dirty parking lot next to the chain link fence surrounding the shipyard. A dingy wooden two-story building squeezed against the broken asphalt of the decaying lot. Across the street, the "Sunshine Tavern" sign sunburned the fog and drizzle electric orange. Eli switched off the motor. The windshield wipers stopped in mid swipe. Eli opened his door and stepped out into the rain. He closed his door, opened the back door and pulled his overcoat out. He closed the door and put the overcoat on, over his already damp sweater. He walked around the car and opened Maggie's door. She stepped out and opened an umbrella.

"This way," he said, and trudged off without waiting for her to follow. She kicked a rusty Coke can out of the way and hurried after him.

They came around the side of the building to the street-side front. Eli stopped and looked up at a window on the second floor. Rain got in his eyes. He walked past the bus stop bench and turned into the building entrance. He pulled open the door and walked into the darkness. Maggie stopped to look at the bus stop bench. A caption reading, 'Welcome to the Emerald City' obscured a picture of the Space Needle with Mount Ranier floating in the background. Maggie followed Eli into the gloom.

Damp wood and curry. Maggie remembered how she felt when she found out she was pregnant with Tom. A wave of nausea enveloped her. She leaned against a wooden banister flowing upward, out of sight. 'Was it stained wood, or just dirty'. She couldn't tell. The single bare light bulb hanging from the ceiling offered little illumination.

Eli stared at the row of rusty mailboxes.

"Apartment 2 C," he said. He rubbed his finger against the plastic name covering, trying to decipher the yellow paper beneath. He tapped against the metal. It rattled, precariously. He pulled out his keys and looked at them. He tried several. None fit.

"Come on," he said, and trudged up the stairs.

Maggie pressed open the door for a quick breath of fresh air and then followed behind, slowly. The walls were dark. The stairs were dark. The floor was dark. She felt like things were hiding in unseen cracks. She shivered in the moldy dampness. The stairs creaked. She could hear muffled sounds behind the gray doors.

Apartment 2 C. Eli tried the doorknob. Locked. He tried it again. Still locked. He rattled it both ways.

"Eli, it's locked, let's go," Maggie pled.

Bam, Bam Bam. Eli shattered the brooding stillness.

He waited.

No response.

Bam, Bam, Bam.

"Anybody home," Eli shouted.

A door, two doors down creaked open a crack. Two eyes peered out of the darkness.

"Of course nobody's home," he said.

Maggie turned to look at the eyes. The door closed.

"Let's go get the Manager," he said and walked back down the stairs. Maggie hurried along behind.

Knock, knock, knock.

"Whadaya want," muffled through the door. The door flew open. A short, fat man with a cigar squeezed out the door. Maggie stepped behind Eli.

"You lookin' for a room," he said, munching the soggy cigar. "We're all full."

"No, I lost my key to 2 C," Eli said.

The fat man squinted at Eli.

"What the hell are you talkin' about?" he said. "You tryin' to break in or somethin'? 'Cause if you is, I'll call the cops. Don't you think I won't."

"No. No. I'm Eli Spellman. I live in 2 C. I can't find my key."

"Like hell you do. You ain't got no key. 'Cause you don't live in 2 C." The fat man liked his rhyme. His yellow teeth showed behind the cigar.

"No really. I'm Eli Spellman. I live in 2 C. I've been gone...for awhile."

"Listen Bub, I been super here for 3 years running. I ain't never heard of no Spellman, and I ain't never seen you, or your old lady."

Rage. Eli grabbed the fat man by the shirt and pushed him up against the door.

"You listen to me 'BUB'. I live in apartment 2 C. And you are going to let me in."

The fat man spit his cigar in Eli's face and shoved him right back. Eli nearly stumbled as he backed into Maggie. Maggie screamed. The fat man seemed pretty used to these kinds of things. He grabbed Eli by the shirt.

"Listen Bub, I don't know what kinda stunt you're tryin' to pull. But you better take your lady friend and get on outta here before I do somethin' you're gonna regret."

"Eli please, let's go," Maggie cried, bracing Eli.

"I live in 2 C," Eli sounded desperate.

The man grabbed Eli by the shirt and railroaded him toward the door, pushing Maggie out of the way. She clutched at Eli, trying to help him. Eli dug his heels in at the door. He brushed the fat man's hands away and pushed him into the banister.

"2 C, I said. 2 C."

"Stop Eli. Stop."

"Let go a me!"

The fat man crashed into the banister and fell to the floor. He clearly hadn't expected so much fight from an old guy.

"Damn it!" he gasped. He tried to knock Eli's legs out from under him. Eli kneeled on his chest.

"I live in apartment 2 C. ARE YOU GOING TO LET ME IN?"

"Eli let him go," Maggie shouted grabbing Eli's arms.

Eli shrugged her hands away.

The fat man rasped his answer.

"What?" Eli shouted.

"Shigai Nokamura lives in 2 C. He's lived there for 20 years."

Stung, Eli repeated, "What?"

"Shigai Nokamura. Get the hell off me."

Eli released his hold on the fat man. The fat man bounced to his feet and prepared for another attack. The fight had gone out of Eli. He looked bewildered.

"I live in 2 C," he whispered.

Maggie put her arms around Eli to steady him.

"Get the hell outta here or I'll press charges," the Fat Man said.

She wiped a drop of blood from Eli's lip, and guided him through the door.

"I ain't never seen ya in my life," the Fat Man called after them.

The cooling rain beaded up on Eli's overcoat, as Maggie guided him into the car. Eli collapsed into the driver's side. Maggie went around and climbed in the passenger side. Eli sat there, breathing hard, staring out the window. Maggie watched him. His breathing slowed.

"Am I crazy Maggie?" he asked.

"No," she said softly.

He turned to look at her. "Then how come I think I lived here for forty years?"

"I don't know Eli. Maybe you dreamed it. Maybe you saw it on TV. Maybe Doc Jones is right. Maybe something happened when you fell."

"Something did happen when I fell. The whole world changed."

"Look at this place Eli. What a nightmare. Let's get outta here."

"Maybe you're right. Maybe it's all just a bad dream," he said. Eli started the car. The windshield wipers cleared the windshield.

"Your umbrella," he said. The fat man had thrown it out the door of the building. It rested upside down by the bus stop, collecting water.

"Leave it," she said.

He looked at her.

"My watch," he said. "How do you explain that?"

"I don't know," she said.

Eli drove out of the parking lot and headed north on 1st avenue.

"Where are we going?" she asked.

"To the Times," he said. "I've got to see Don Morgan."

"Who's Don Morgan?"

"My old boss."

"Eli?"

"I know. It's crazy. But I have to Mag. If there is no Don Morgan, I'll give this whole thing up. I'll accept my new...our life, and I'll never mention the Times again."

"Promise?" she asked.

"I'm not crazy Maggie. I'm not getting senile. It just seemed so real."

No response.

"And I can't remember anything else," he continued. "How do you explain that?"

"A bump on the head."

"Right!"

"No seriously Eli. Before you fell off that ladder, we'd been talking about a trip to Seattle. Our second honeymoon. Somehow, you mixed all this in, when you fell. That's all."

Eli drove under the Viaduct, and took Alaskan Way to the waterfront.

"Maybe," he said.

CHAPTER THIRTEEN

THEY DROVE SLOWLY PAST the Ferry terminal, slowly, because that was the only thing they could do. The traffic leading into the Ferry terminal was horrendous. Eli was in the wrong lane.

"I think," Maggy said, "if we stay in this lane, we'll end up on the Bremerton Ferry."

The green, Washington State Ferry sign floated in the mist above the street, pointing to the left, Bremerton Ferry. Eli slowed to a stop behind the car in front. He switched on his right blinker and looked over his shoulder. No where to go.

"Come on," he said. "Let me in."

He forced his way into the right lane and avoided entering the terminal. Piers and shops held back Puget Sound, on the left. Concrete pillars, holding up the viaduct, also held back the rapidly sloping hills on the right. A green and gold trolley train wormed its way past them, under the cover of the viaduct. They continued north on Alaskan way.

"Where is the Times?" Maggy asked.

"It should be up here just a little ways past pier 72," Eli said. "We'll have to park under the viaduct and pay the meter. That's another reason why I never liked to drive."

Eli turned right on Seneca street, crossing the Trolley tracks, and then turned left, under the concrete shelter of the viaduct. He pulled into a parking stall and shut off the motor.

"You want to come, or you want to wait here?" he asked.

Maggy looked around.

"Where is it?" she asked.

"Two blocks up the street," he pointed.

"I'll come," she said.

"It's wet," he said.

Maggy opened her door and got out. Eli did the same. He walked around to the front of the car and looked at the parking meter. He felt in his pants pocket. Empty.

"Change?" Maggy said, holding up two quarters.

"Fifteen minutes for twenty five cents," Eli said.

"Not much time," Maggy said.

Eli dropped the quarters in the slot.

"Better hurry," she said.

He pulled his overcoat closed and crossed the Trolley tracks. She did the same.

They walked north along the street to the first crosswalk. Wind off the bay, carried water pellets in each gust. It pushed against them as they crossed to the waterfront side of the street, nearly tumbling into the shelter of the shops. The retail shops dissolved into corrugated tin buildings as they moved northward through the mist. Eli stopped in front of a graying worm-wood building with a rusty roof. Bewildered. He looked up and down the waterfront with that 'there must be more' look in his eyes. Maggy stepped up against the side of the building to avoid the falling water. A weathered old homeless man seemed to materialize against the grayness of the building, startling Maggy. She stepped back into the rain, next to Eli.

"What happened to the Times?" Eli asked the old man.

The old man held up a cardboard sign. Painted red letters displayed, '2 Tim 3:1-3'.

Eli scoffed. "Crazy old goat! Let's go Maggy."

Maggy pulled some more change out of her purse and handed it to the old man.

"V'you got the time?" the Old Man asked.

Eli felt in his pocket for his watch.

"No!" Eli said, pulling Maggy with him as he walked away.

"'Sa'shame," the Old Man muttered, as they walked away.

"Now What," Eli thought, as he walked. "I really am crazy."

They passed a sidewalk seafood café.

"I'm hungry," Maggy said. "Let's get some lunch Eli."

The warm smell of fish and chips wafted on the damp breeze. Eli's stomach growled.

"Okay," he said, and they got in line.

He looked at the stained-aproned-kid behind the counter, taking people's money. Above his head was a sign. IVAR'S ACRES OF CLAMS.

"Ivar's. That was the street," he said.

"What?" Maggy said.

"Maybe it really was dream," he said.

They got to the front.

"What'll it be?" the kid said.

"Fish and Chips," Maggy said.

"Clams and Chips," Eli said.

"Drinks," the kid said.

"Root beer," Eli said.

"Do you have any hot chocolate?" Maggy asked.

"You bet," the kid said. "That'll be $13.50."

"Say, kid. Do you happen to know where the Seattle Times building is?" Eli asked, handing him a twenty.

"No clue," the kid said, filling paper dishes with deep fried bits.

"How about Ivar street?" Eli said.

"Nope," the kid said. "Change." The kid handed Eli some bills and some quarters. "Enjoy," he said handing them their lunch.

"Thanks," Maggy said.

"Next," the kid said.

Maggy and Eli walked around the side of Ivar's Acres of Clams. The café was built on a pier, over the

water. They had put tables along the outside of the building for people to sit and eat, outdoors. The eaves of the roof covered about half of the table. Maggy and Eli sat down opposite each other and scrunched against the building to keep from getting dripped on. The view of Eliot bay was constrained by the steely gray clouds, sitting heavy on the water. The great Green and White Bremerton Ferry belched three times and launched itself into the swirling mist. A young boy stood against the black railing overlooking a tugboat dock below. He held a french-fry in his hand, statue-of-liberty like. A white-on-gray seagull materialized out the clouds on a swooping dive and snatched the french-fry out of the boys hand. The boy laughed delightedly and turned to his parents.

"Again," he said.

Another french-fry disappeared as a streak of white shot past.

"Isn't that wonderful?" Maggy said.

No response. Eli wondered what happened to the seagull after it dropped below the pier.

* * *

When they made it back to their car, they met Rico, the meter man. He was just placing a $35 parking ticket on their windshield. Eli ran to stop him, leaving Maggy to drift in.

"We were just leaving," Eli said, grabbing the ticket off the windshield and trying to give it back to Rico.

"Sorry man. I already signed it. Nothing I can do," Rico said. He climbed in his shrunken go-truck.

"Wait!" Eli cried.

Rico hesitated.

"Do you know where the Times building is?" Eli said.

"Two blocks up. Four blocks over. 'Cross from the Center. Spinning Globe on top." Rico puttered away.

"That's it," Eli exclaimed. "Let's go."

Eli stopped in front of the large glass doors of the Seattle Times building.

The Large Globe set atop the building spun one day for every half hour, oblivious to the shadow it cast over entrants into building. Eli looked in the glass. Maggy stared back at him, by his side.

"This is it," he said, looking in. In the glass, he could see she nodded. He opened the door and stepped through it. She held the door open, and then followed him in. His feet squeaked on the marble floor. Hers clicked. They crossed the cavernous entrance.

"Seattle Times. How may I direct your call?"

Click.

"Seattle Times. How may I direct your call?"

Click.

Eli and Maggy stepped up to the granite counter reception chamber.

"May I help you?" the head-set clad, tight-lipped woman said.

"Is Don Morgan in?" Eli asked.

The woman held up a bony finger.

"Seattle Times. How may I direct your call?"

Click. "Do you have an appointment?" she asked.

"No," Eli said.

"Seattle Times. How may I direct your call?"

Click. "Name."

"Spellman. Eli Spellman...Oh, and Maggy."

"I'll see if Mr. Morgan is in. Seattle Times. How may I direct you call?"

Click. Beepbeepbeepbeep.

"See Maggy, there is a Don Morgan," Eli said.

"Hi Shirley, this is Daidre. How are ya?...Yes...I did..."

Daidre touched the corner of her mouth.

"You are?...You should do it...For sure..."

She patted the bags under her eyes.

"Oh, those cucumbers feel so nice and cool...I was there for about an hour..."

Eli coughed.

"Oh, hey Shirley, I've got a..."

She looked at a note pad, Eli hadn't noticed she'd written on.

"...Mr. and Ms. Spellman here to see Don...I dunno...I'll see."

Click.

"Why do you want to see Mr. Morgan?" Daidre asked.

"I used to work here," Eli said.

Click.

"Shirley, he says he used to work here...Okay...You betcha...bubye."

Click.

"Seattle Times. How may I direct your call?"

Click.

"Seattle Times. How may I direct your call?"

Click.

Eli coughed again. Daidre flapped her hand at the elevator.

"Please have a seat. I'll letcha know. Seattle Times. How may I direct your call?"

Click.

Eli and Maggy looked toward the elevator and followed the breeze created by Daidre's hand, to a couple of steel frame office chairs. 'Seattle Times. How may I direct your call? Click,' continued to drone. They sat down.

Breeeeeeeeep.

"Oh hi Shirley...he will...you're kidding...uh uh...uh uh...uh uh...Okey dokey...bubye. Seattle Times. How may I direct your call?"

Click.

Daidre stood up and shouted across the cavernous room. "Mr. Morgan will see you now. Third floor, on the left." She flapped her hand at the ceiling and sat down. "Seattle Times. How may I direct your call?"

Eli and Maggy stood up and pressed the Up button on the elevator. It opened. They stepped in. Eli pressed the 3 button. The door closed.

"Who's Don Morgan?" Maggy asked.

"Just a kid," Eli said. "He used to be my...I think...I thought...he used to be my boss."

"Oh," Maggy said. "At least there is a Don Morgan."

The door opened. They stepped out. Eli looked to his left, down a row of gray office cubicles. More drones with headsets created a cacophony of sound. The one-sided conversations were unintelligible. They walked down the row, looking for Don Morgan.

"The office down there," Eli pointed to the end of the row. Maggy followed him. They stepped into the office. A rather plump woman, dressed in designer pink, stood up to greet them.

"You must be Mr. Spellman, and Ms. Spellman," she said. "I'm Shirley, Mr. Morgan's administrative assistant." She shook their hands.

"We've heard so much about you," Maggy said. "I feel like I know you already."

"Really," Shirley smiled a pink smile, if that were possible. "Well, anyway, Mr. Morgan is the managing editor of the Lifestyle Section for both the Seattle Times, and the Seattle Post Intelligencer. He is a very busy man. Believe you me." She giggled. "I can hardly believe he has agreed to meet with you. But, he has. And he is. So here we are." She giggled.

"Thank you very much," Eli said.

She giggled. The inner office door opened. A tall, distinguished looking man, with dark hair, graying at the temples stepped out of the office.

"Mr. Morgan," Shirley said. "May I present Mr. and Ms. Spellman. They're here to see you. I'm not really sure why. But they are." She giggled. "Why are you here to see Mr. Morgan?" she asked.

"That's quite alright Shirley," Mr. Morgan said. She giggled. "Mr. and 'Ms.' Is it?" Mr. Morgan asked warmly.

"Mrs," Maggy said.

"Spellman," Eli said.

Don Morgan extended a firm handshake to them both. Eli's face had lost its color.

"Come in. Come into my office. What can I do for you?" Mr. Morgan asked.

"Are you alright?" he asked Eli, as they sat down around the coffee table of his spacious office. Maggy and Eli sat down. Mr. Morgan poured a drink of golden liquid into a mug.

"Here, have some apple cider," he said to Eli. "Lifestyles doing a feature on the Fall Harvest Festival. It's pretty good stuff. But I'm sure you know that already. Right? Spellman farms?"

Mr. Morgan showed them the Spellman Farms logo, printed on the label of the cider bottle.

"That is why you're here to see me. Isn't it?" he said.

Eli didn't believe in ghosts. He'd never thought much about Déjà vu. Maybe what he could remember was what was going to happen. Not what had happened. But, he remembered Don Morgan, not this Don Morgan, saying that same thing to him. Mechanically, he accepted the drink. Don poured another for Maggy.

"Thank you," she said. "You're very kind." Maggy was watching Eli.

"Not at all," Mr. Morgan said. "It's a privilege to have the Patriarch and Matriarch of the Spellman Farm legacy in my office. Your farm will be featured prominently in our Harvest Festival piece next week."

Maggy returned Mr. Morgan's compliments with a warm smile.

"Thank you very much," she said.

Eli stared at Don Morgan, blankly, and shifted uncomfortably in his seat. Don leaned forward to engage Eli.

"So, don't worry Mr. Spellman. We're not going to do an expose on the side effects of chemical treatment on Washington Apples." Mr. Morgan laughed heartily. Maggy laughed, uncomfortably. Eli jumped up and paced behind his chair.

"Eli!" Maggy said.

Don Morgan stood up.

"I'm sorry. I was only joking," he said.

Eli stopped pacing and stared directly at Don Morgan.

"Did I ever work for you?" he said.

"What?" Don asked.

Maggy stood up and held her breath.

"Did I ever work for you?" Eli bored.

"Why, no," Don said. "Of course not. I asked one of our reporters to do a sketch on your operation. I assume that's why you're here. He did contact you didn't he? Manuel Ortega. Young guy. Late twenties."

"Do you know Alden Blethen?" Eli drilled.

"Say, who's the reporter here anyway. What's this all about?" Don asked, loosing his smile.

"Do you know Alden Blethen?" Eli repeated.

Don sat on the edge of his desk and crossed his arms. "Of course I know who Alden Blethen is. Everybody at the Times knows who Alden Blethen is."

"Did he give me this watch?" Eli pulled the watch from his pocket and held it out for Don to see. Don took a step closer for a better view. Maggy looked closely too.

"It's broken," Don said.

"Open it up," Eli commanded. He gave the watch to Don. Don tried to open the cover. His fingers slipped. He stuck his fingernail in between the face cover and the watch and pried it open. He looked carefully.

"Crystal's cracked," he said.

"Read it. Read the inscription," Eli said. Don read:

"Time does not change us. It just unfolds us."

"Did Alden Blethen give me this watch as a retirement gift?" Eli asked.

Don held the watch. He turned it over in his hand. He gave it back to Eli.

"Alden Blethen founded the Seattle Times," Don said. "He died in 1915."

CHAPTER FOURTEEN

ELI OPENED THE PASSENGER side of the aging Pontiac and gave the keys to Maggy.

"You drive," he said. He climbed in. Maggy stood outside the passenger door.

"Eli," she protested, "I haven't driven this way in forty years."

"You know the way," he said, and pulled the door closed.

Maggy stared in the passenger window. Eli was gray in the interior shadows. Maggy walked around the back of the car and climbed into the driver's seat. She turned the key. The old car coughed, sputtered, and came to life. She looked both ways, then pulled out into traffic.

"I don't know this city like you do," she said as they drove past Ivar's. Eli turned and looked at her, coldly, but said nothing. They stopped at a red light. The sign overhead pointed in three directions, I-90, I-5, West Seattle Freeway.

"Which way do I go?" she said.

"That way," he pointed straight ahead.

Maggy got on the I-90 headed east. Home.

Eli leaned his head back against the seat and closed his eyes.

* * *

The rains had stopped. The puffy clouds bounced heavily off the rugged hills surrounding Seattle as Maggy crossed the floating bridge. Lake Washington reflected the broken gray sky and green black forested hills. An occasional blue eye peeked through a hole in the sky. Maggy liked the contrast.

"Do you think I'm crazy," Eli said. Maggy started. She didn't know what she thought. Well, that wasn't true. She did think there was something wrong. Eli's erratic behavior worried her sick. Not really sick. But like that feeling you get in your stomach after going upside down and backwards on the roller coaster. The thing was, the feeling wasn't going away. Eli kept bringing it up. Every time he did, she took another turn. After enough turns, you lost your lunch. Maybe now they'd been to Seattle, she could get off the ride.

"No," she said.

"I won't mention it again," he said. Her stomach did another loop.

"Good," she said. They drove for awhile in silence.

"Talk to me Maggy," he said. "Tell me all the things I missed."

"What do you mean," she said.

He looked over at her. "I don't know. I don't remember."

"Well...Tom and Andy pretty much have things under control for the Festival next week. Tom was hoping that you'd man the cider booth on Saturday. Everyone's coming to dinner this Sunday. Wilma's cooking the turkey. Marci's bringing the salad. Sarah said she'd make rolls, but I told her I'd do it instead. I don't want her on her feet anymore than she has to. She really has me worried. Marci's making the pies. I'm doing the stuffing. I said I thought we ought to get the girls involved in cooking after school. Kids these days. Seems to me that cooking's a dying art. Let's see, Myrna asked

me to help out with the bazaar. I'm donating three dozen jars of apple butter. That reminds me. I need to pick up some more mason jars in Salem, before

Tuesday. Jaren has a football game tonight. We said we'd go watch, if we were back in time. What else? I'll have to look at my calendar when we get home."

Maggy ran out of events. Eli just enjoyed hearing her voice.

"Us," he said. "Tell me about us."

"Us." She laughed. "We just are."

"No really Mag...what about us."

"Tom and Andy run the farm, Eli. They're doing a fine job. Ken runs the business. Wilma and Marci help me all the time, and Sarah's still in the baby business. They all try to make us feel like we're needed Eli. But I know what this is all about." She stopped suddenly. Traffic bunched up ahead. The sun came out. She started again.

"What?" Eli said.

"We're old," she said. "They don't need us anymore. That's what this is all about, isn't it?"

Eli thought about it. He couldn't remember.

"Maybe," he said. "Could be," he thought. He didn't know anymore.

They drove in silence for a time.

"Us," he said. "You didn't tell me about us."

She laughed. "I told you. We're old."

"I know that," he said. "Tell me something I don't know."

"For instance?" she said.

"Okay," he smiled. "Tell me about when I was young and handsome, and you were just as beautiful as you are now."

"Pretty smooth, for a farmer, don't ya think?" she said smiling. "Hopin' to get lucky?"

His face colored, noticeably. His heart beat faster. So did hers.

"Maybe," he said, looking away.

"Why Mr. Spellman. Is that a proposition?" she said with a smirk.

Eli didn't look at her.

"Tell me Maggy. Tell me about us. Make it up if you have to."

So, she did. She began slowly. She told him about growing up together. Falling in love. What she thought when he proposed. What she wore when they

got married. How she felt when she found out she was pregnant the first time.

Eli listened to the sound of her voice. He laid his head back against the seat and closed his eyes. The sound of her voice told the stories of their lives. His dreams filled in the blanks. He saw her as he never had before. He saw the births. He saw the deaths. He saw their interconnectedness. It seemed like they had always been together. It seemed like they could, or should, or would, always be together. Her voice wove the fabric of their lives so tightly, he could not see the individual threads. They were one cloth, inseparable. And, the design of the fabric was spectacular. But it was not complete. There was something missing. What was it? He couldn't see it. The cloth draped off the end of the table. Just a little ways off the table. If he could just pull it towards him a bit, he could see the rest of the design.

CHAPTER FIFTEEN

"GRANDPA, WAKE UP," EMY SAID.

Eli pulled harder on the cloth. He wanted to see the rest of the design. Someone pulled back. The design changed. The colors faded. He was pulling a rope. Tug-o-war. He wasn't winning. The rope was slippery. He couldn't hold on. A bridge. It was raining. He was pulling. He fell. Deep water. Someone was pounding on the window. His head was pounding. He couldn't breath. He gasped for air and reached for her hands.

"Grampa, it's time to go," Emy said, knocking on the car window.

Eli gasped and sat up, disoriented. The water drained away. Eli tried to see who was reaching for him in the half-light of dusk.

"Hurry Grampa. The game starts in twenty minutes," Emy said, opening the door of the old Pontiac.

"What game?" Eli said, still not sure where he was.

"Jaren's game, silly," Emy said.

Eli swung his legs around and felt for solid ground. "Jaren," he thought. "I know that name." Somewhere, he remembered hearing the name. He just couldn't quite place it.

"Hi sleepy head," Maggy said, stepping down off the porch steps. "Enjoy your nap?" Maggy was followed by Tom and Wilma carrying Pendleton wool blankets and a cooler.

"No," Eli snapped. His neck hurt. His back hurt. The dryness in his throat told him he'd probably been lying there with his mouth wide open. Who knew what could have gone in there, or come out, for that matter. He stood up. His knees were stiff.

"I tried to wake you," Maggy said, with that 'I told you so' attitude. "But you were sleeping so soundly, we all decided to let you sleep. Sweet dreams?"

Tom opened the back of a Ford Explorer and tossed the blankets in. Eli rubbed the back of his neck. Emy reached in grabbed a hat off the back seat.

"Here grandpa, sit by me," she handed Eli the hat and jumped in the back seat of the Explorer. He ran his hands through his bent gray hair, as he looked at the hat. 'Salem Valley Chiefs'.

"Here's your coat. It's likely to get pretty cold tonight," Maggy said, following

Emy in. "Slide over Hon," she said.

"I want to sit by Grandpa," Emy said.

"Slide all the way over Emy," Wilma said.

"It's alright," Maggy said. "Climb over me and sit in the middle."

Tom opened the passenger door and Wilma climbed in, still holding a small cooler. Emy scuffled over Maggy to sit in the middle seat.

"Buckle up," Maggy said.

"Hop in, Dad," Tom said, coming around to the driver's side.

Eli watched the proceedings with his feet planted firmly. Everything seemed so natural to them, like it had all happened many times before. With great effort, he moved his feet and climbed in for the ride.

* * *

Tom pulled the SUV into the High School parking lot, as the marching band marched past. Eli thought it

sounded like they were playing 'On Wisconsin', but he was sure that wasn't right. He could see across the flat parking lot, to the flat field. Two teams were practicing at opposite ends. The bleacher seats were filling with colored swatches. Andy and Marci waved them into an empty parking stall right next to a hibachi barbecue. Ken Chapman speared hotdogs off the barbecue and handed them to, what seemed to Eli, a crowd of small urchins. Emy couldn't hold still. Maggy opened her door and Emy burst out, into the line for hotdogs.

"Hungry?" Maggy asked.

The smell of barbecued hotdogs and charcoal wafted through the SUV. Eli's stomach growled. He was hungry. He just didn't know if it was hotdogs he was hungry for.

Tom and Wilma got out and mixed in seamlessly. Maggy climbed out.

"Hi Mom. How's Dad?" Marci said, as if Eli couldn't hear, or wasn't there.

That was fine with Eli though. He knew she was talking about him. But, he felt detached from this rather chaotic family gathering.

"He's just fine dear," Maggy said, turning and motioning for Eli to get out. "Where's Sarah?"

Eli got out of the SUV and came around to stand behind Maggy, maintaining his distance.

"She was just too tired," Marci said.

"Hi Mom, Dad," Ken said, handing Maggy a hotdog. "I think she needs to stay down, even if it is homecoming. Want one Dad?"

Ken handed a hotdog to Eli without waiting for a response.

"Chips and sodas are in the back of my truck," Andy said. "I think there's some left."

"Hits the spot," Maggy said, taking a bite of her hotdog.

"Better eat fast," Marci said.

"Game starts in about 5 minutes," Andy said.

"Hurry and eat Emy," Wilma said.

"Where's Jenny and Mary and Chloe?" Emy asked.

"They're saving our seats," Marci said.

"This way everyone," Tom said, in his best shepherd voice.

Surprisingly, Eli thought, they all followed. It was homecoming.

CHAPTER SIXTEEN

MAGGY PULLED THE QUILTED BED cover off the bed and gently laid it over the rocking chair in the corner, as Eli came out of the bathroom. He leaned against the bathroom doorframe and watched her. Her cheeks colored as he stared. She turned back the down comforter.

"Great game tonight, wasn't it?" she said, fluffing the pillows.

Eli thought her movements were full of grace, if the fluffing of pillows could ever be considered graceful. It was not what she was doing, but how she did it that intrigued Eli. Her loose cotton robe trailed her lightly, as she came around the bed.

"Yep," Eli said, watching her carefully. Maggy looked up, catching him in his stare. Eli looked away. Maggy smiled.

"Jaren played well," Maggy said, turning down Eli's corner of the bed.

"Yep," Eli said, returning his gaze to her movements.

Eli really had enjoyed the evening. He was a football fan. Jaren had played a good game. It had taken Eli the entire first quarter to figure out who Jaren was, without asking anyone in this family that he was inextricably attached to, but hardly knew. Now though, he wasn't thinking about football. Neither was Maggy.

"My turn," she said, lightly, approaching the bathroom door.

Eli didn't move out of the doorway. He smiled. Her eyes sparkled. She pressed against him. He could feel the shape of her body beneath her cotton robe, and nightgown. Together, they turned, like a joint valve, opening. She lingered, shape fitting shape. She smiled, and slid into the bathroom. Eli sat down on the edge of the bed, as the bathroom door closed. He slid out of his slippers, swung his legs up on the bed, and floated deep into the fluffed pillows and down comforter. He heard the faucet turn on in the bathroom. Maggy was humming. What was the tune? 'Love Me Tender'? The comforter was cool on his feet. The sound of water running grew louder. He felt the tension flowing out of his body. He was floating. Softly. Gently. The water was warm. It seemed to envelop him. He was moving. Downstream or up? He couldn't tell. He could see a bridge in the distance. Was it moving closer, or getting further away? In the dim light of evening, he couldn't tell. Did it matter? The water was warm. The sound carried him.

Maggy opened the bathroom door and leaned against the doorframe, in just her nightgown, striking a pose.

"Feeling lucky?" she said, in a whispered husky voice.

Eli answered with a snort, then a quick snore.

"Oh Eli," Maggy said softly. The intensity of the day's emotions drained out of her. She was empty and exhausted. Alone and lonely. Quietly, she padded around to her side of the bed. She switched off the light and gently climbed into bed, next to the man she had been sleeping with for nearly forty years.

CHAPTER SEVENTEEN

"DO YOU THINK YOU COULD show me how this thing works, Emy?" Eli said, standing before an old apple cider press.

"Sure Grandpa," Emy said, anxious to be involved.

Eli was especially grateful for the little girl's willingness, seeing as how he really wasn't all that sure how the press worked.

"Like this," Emy said, taking her place in front of the flywheel. She gave the wheel a valiant turn. It turned slowly, then stopped. Emy looked disappointed. She stood on her tiptoes and looked over the edge of the tin hopper.

"It's not working," she said.

"Let me give it a try," Eli said, collaboratively.

He stepped closer and spun the cast-iron flywheel on the old cider press like a helmsman turning hard to starboard. The spinning grinder, inside the hopper hummed. Emy smiled.

"Okay Emy," he said. "Pour 'em in."

Little Emy could barely lift the bushel basket of apples high enough to pour them in the tin hopper. Eli helped her out, lifting her up. Hand on hand, Grandfather and granddaughter tipped the basket and apples tumbled into the hopper. The grinder slowed to a halt as the apples rattled around in the hopper. Eli let go of the basket and gave the flywheel another spin. Apple mash began to drop from the grinder into the press.

"It's working Grandpa," Emy said.

Eli smiled. Hand over hand, he turned the flywheel. Emmy watched with anxious eyes.

"Can I have some Grandpa?" Emy asked.

Eli continued to spin the flywheel, breathing a little hard against the effort.

"Not yet, little one," he said. "We haven't pressed yet. Besides, if you drink all the cider, what are we gonna serve all these tourists?" Eli motioned with his head to the crowded street, beyond their barn-like display booth.

The Fall Harvest Festival had just begun in Salem, and Spellman Farms was certainly one of the highlights. They had created a long, three wall barn-like booth, for displaying their wares, their crafts, and their skills. The whole family was involved. The display was divided in sections; all about apples, harvesting, cooking, juicing, and of course, a section where you could purchase their home made apple products. In one section, Maggie and Sarah were tantalizing the town with the aroma of freshly baked apple tarts, and apple pies. Wilma and Marci were selling jams, jellies and vinegars faster than Andy and Ken could keep them stocked. Tom was talking with town council members and other dignitaries about the season's harvest, taxes, and town improvements. Jaren and Jenny, the Spellman teens were the gophers. Anything the adults needed, Jaren and Jenny were called upon to do. The small Spellmans, cousins, were out harassing other vendors, eating free samples, or playing at the various games set up throughout the street fair Harvest Festival. Everybody loved the Festival, except Jenny. This was her first year to help man the booths full-time. She wanted to be out with her friends, listening to the blue grass players, eating cotton candy and playing games.

"More Cider Grandpa," Jenny relayed from the women folk.

"Coming right up," he answered. "Okay Emy, what next?"

Emy pointed to the press screw on top of the press.

Eli wiped the sweat from his forehead and turned the cider press screw a quarter turn. Emy squatted down close to watch. Golden juice began to flow into an empty cask from the spigot attached to the oak barrel containing the mushy apple pomace. Eli turned the screw another quarter turn. The flow increased.

"Faster Grandpa," Jenny said. "Grandma says they can't serve hot apple pie without fresh juice."

"Hold your horses," Eli said. "If I turn too fast, you'll be drinking the dregs. Grandma won't like that either."

"Oooh yuck," Emy said.

A small crowd had gathered to watch as Eli turned the cider press screw. The fresh golden apple juice was flowing from the press in a mouth-watering stream. The wooden cask was nearly full. Eli looked at the crowd and smiled.

"If you want a drink, you'll have to move on down there to the Missus. Me, I just squeeze the stuff," Eli said, playing to the crowd. Several chuckles were heard.

"Jaren, come take this keg down to Grandma."

"Sure thing, Grandpa," Jaren said, hopping into action.

Eli reached down and shut off the spigot. Jaren lifted the cask, sloshing the freshly squeezed juice.

"Careful now son. I worked too hard for you to be leavin' any of that juice on the ground." Eli winked at the gathering. They laughed outright. Jaren smiled and made off with the cask, and with most of the crowd.

Eli reached into the oak press and lifted a wet, sticky, very heavy press bag, containing the apple mash. He emptied the mushy contents of the press bag into a plastic bucket, behind the cider press and leaned against the flywheel to rest for a moment. He had thought a lot about the Harvest Festival during the past week. It was enjoyable to watch the entire family, his family, work together to prepare for such an event. And, he really was enjoying himself. He'd learned more about apples in the last week than he thought could ever be learned. It made Eli feel good when Tom told Sarah at dinner the other night that Grandpa, Dad, had forgotten more about the apple harvest than most farmers would ever know. Eli knew that was Tom's good-natured approach to explaining away Eli's recent erratic behavior. Eli could see that Tom did have a way of pulling the family together. In the past week, he had gotten used to the idea of family. And, since he now had a family, it was nice having a son to take care of things. It was also nice knowing that it made Maggie feel so much better. Maggie. Eli looked at this aging woman, so beautiful, so full of life and wondered why she didn't see right through him.

"Mr. Spellman?"

Deep in thought, Eli placed the press bag back inside the cider press, apparently not hearing his name called. He reached down, under the wooden shelf behind the press and extracted a new cheese cloth press liner.

"Mr. Spellman?"

"That'd be me," he said, not looking back.

"Mr. Spellman, I'm Manuel Ortega from the Seattle Times Lifestyle Section."

The good-naturedness Eli had been feeling all morning at the Harvest Festival dried up in an instant.

"I believe you spoke to Don Morgan, my editor," Manuel continued. "I'd like to interview the Patriarch of Spellman farms." Manuel smiled and reached out to shake hands.

Eli clasped Manuel's hand and looked him in the eye. Manuel had deep brown eyes, close cropped black hair and light brown skin. Eli held his grip, uncomfortably long.

"Do I know you?" Eli asked.

Manuel's smile grew a little bit bigger. "Well, some people tell me I look a lot like Emilio Estevez."

Eli smiled back and released Manuel's hand. "The kid has a pretty good self image," Eli thought. He obviously didn't look anything like Emilio Estevez.

"Do you know me?" Eli questioned.

"No," Manuel said. "But I've heard an awful lot about you."

"That right?" Eli said.

"Mind if I ask you a few questions?" Manuel said.

"Listen Manuel, somehow I got roped into a shift here at the cider press. My shift won't be over for another hour. If I don't crank out the ider, Mrs. Spellman won't be too happy, see." Eli nodded toward the women making pies, down the row. Manuel followed his gaze, as he took in the extent of the Spellman Farms Family Harvest Festival show. "Besides," Eli continued, "I know just enough to be dangerous. Tom's the one you want to talk with. He's runnin' the show now."

Manuel had taken a pencil and pad of paper out of his Eddie Bauer jacket and was making some notes.

"How 'bout if I take a few pictures while you work? That way I can get some action shots," Manuel pressed.

"Suit yerself," Eli exaggerated a country drawl. "Got another bushel for me Emy?"

"You bet Grandpa," Emy said.

Again, Grandfather and Granddaughter poured the bushel basket of apples into the tin hopper.

"That's great," Manuel exclaimed. "Could you hold it right there?"

Emy smiled a big smile. She wanted to be a star. Eli scowled. Manuel snapped a picture.

"Tell me this, Mr. Spellman," Manuel said, "how did you get into farming apples."

Eli spun the flywheel. The apple pomace began to dribble out of the grinder.

"Good question," Eli said. "I don't rightly know. I guess I just fell into it."

Manuel laughed. Eli was serious.

"Come on," Manuel said. "How long have you been doing this?"

Eli stopped spinning the flywheel and squinted at the sun. "Somedays, it seems like I just started. Most days, I just can't remember."

Manuel smiled. Eli was not an easy interview.

"You must really love what you do," Manuel said.

Eli looked over at Maggie. "You wanna know something Manuel?" Eli paused.

"What?" Manuel prodded.

Eli looked back at Manuel.

"Lately I've realized, there is nothing I would rather be doing." Eli looked at the young reporter and then turned the Cider Press screw a quarter turn. Manuel scribbled rapidly in his notepad. Juice began to flow from the spigot. Eli turned the screw another quarter.

"Emy," Eli said. "Would you please hand me a Spellman Farms mug?"

Emy pulled a mug off the shelf behind the Cider Press and handed it to Eli. Eli placed the mug in the Cider stream and filled the mug.

"Care for a mug of fresh apple cider?" Eli said, holding the mug out to Manuel. "Lifestyle section's coverage won't be complete unless you taste what we have to offer."

"You bet," Manuel said, taking the mug. Eli watched him anxiously. Manuel took a drink.

"Well?" Eli asked.

Manuel smacked his lips. "Ummm. This is really good."

Eli let out a breath. Only the careful observer would have realized he had been holding it.

"That's just what I think," Eli said reflectively. "Kinda makes you never want to leave."

Manuel looked at Eli a little strangely, and took another drink. Eli put his arm around the young man's shoulder and began to usher him down to the other end of the long display.

"Jaren," Eli called. "Take over for me, will you?"

Jaren jumped up. "Sure thing Grandpa."

"Great kid," Eli said. "Now Manuel, if you really want to know about Spellman Farms, you need to talk with Tom, my...son. He can tell you all about it."

Eli winked at Maggie as they walked by.

"I've got some hot apple pie here...with ice cream," she smiled seductively at both men.

"See what I mean," Eli said.

Manuel smiled at the old couple. He wasn't sure what he would write, but he was getting the flavor.

"Tom," Eli said, as they approached a small group of men. "This here's Manuel Ortega, from the Seattle Times. Lifestyle's doing a piece on us. Manuel needs more information than I can possibly give."

Tom shook hands with one of the men in his group, and stepped away. He reached out and shook Manuel's hand, warmly.

"Manuel," Tom said. "Glad to meet you. I heard you were coming."

"Nice to meet you," Manuel said.

"There you go," Eli said. "Tom'll take care of you. I best be getting back to my post. Tom here's a slave driver."

"No rest for the wicked," Tom said.

"That'd be me," Eli said, winking at Manuel. "Anytime you want a little flavor, without the substance, you come talk to me." Eli slapped Manuel on the shoulder and sauntered off.

Manuel watched, smiling, as Eli passed by the apple pie display. Maggie held out a fork with a bite of hot pie. Eli stopped and Maggie placed the bite deliciously in Eli's mouth. Manuel looked envious.

"Life must be interesting with him around," Manuel chuckled.

"You have no idea," Tom said.

CHAPTER EIGHTEEN

THE INDIAN-SUMMER SUN WAS just dipping below the Cascade peaks to the east. Ribbons of red and gold and orange and magenta ran along an evening sky, decorating the Salem Harvest Festival. A swelling moon filled a rich purple sky to the east. Eli and Maggie strolled among the street vendors, eating ice cream, and enjoying the late season warmth.

"Red sky at night," Maggie said, holding Eli's hand.

"Sailors' delight," Eli finished.

Many of the shops in the town square were closing, with the onset of nightfall. However, the teenagers were coming out in force, as the night-time entertainment began to come alive. There were cloggers on the main stage in the town square thundering their steps in the clear night air. Blue grass players were strumming and picking and fiddling around town. A square dance caller's voice sashayed through the night sky, inviting couples to dosie-doe on by. And, from somewhere, probably farther away than the volume would indicate, a country-rock band reverberated, sympathetically, among the youth. The town was filled with energy.

Despite the fact that Eli and Maggie had been working the festival most of the day, they were energized by its sounds and smells and life.

"Isn't it grand?" Maggie said, as they stopped to toe tap with a blue grass band. Eli licked a drip from his ice cream cone, not quite finding his rhythm to 'Foggy Mountain Breakdown'. Maggie watched a young man grab his girl by the waist and begin a country swing that sent both boy and girl spinning and laughing to the guitar and mandolin solo. Maggie clapped her hands with enthusiasm.

"Oh Eli, remember when?" she said, watching the couple.

Eli smiled, sadly, but didn't speak. Maggie turned to look at him. She squeezed his hand, realizing her error.

"I'm sorry," she said. "I didn't..."

"It's alright," he interrupted. "I never was much of a dancer."

They walked on, content to let the growing sounds of night, blend with the crowds and music. Maggie enjoyed window shopping in the town square, away from the crowds. Eli was content to watch Maggie. Neither spoke for some time.

"Let's sit a spell," Eli said, taking advantage of a wrought iron bench in the town square.

They sat down, facing west, and watched the last auburn rays of the setting sun change to deep purple. The evening star shone bright on the horizon. Another star woke up. Then another. Eli looked for the north star.

"Still too light," Maggie said, following Eli's gaze. "Give it time."

"It's out there alright," Eli said. "I just can't see it yet."

"You will," she said.

"If I wait long enough," he said.

"Whadya think of the Festival today?" she said.

"Amazing," he said.

"What do you mean?"

"Just amazing," he said. "This whole family working together like that." He hesitated.

She waited for him.

"It's like...something...to hold onto. Something worth holding onto." He stopped, not quite able to put into words what he felt.

She smiled.

"I mean," he started again, "Tom's great. He had those politicians eating out of his hand. And that reporter from the Times. I knew I needed to get him away from me as quick as possible. And Andy and Ken. They really know the business. Jaren and Jenny, they worked harder than anyone. And you. You and the girls. Not only are you beautiful and talented, but, you know how to feed an army. Unbelievable. I've never seen anything like it. How do you do it?"

He talked himself out.

"It's just our family," she whispered.

He looked again at the night sky. The big dipper was just appearing. He shivered, feeling all of the day's energy drain out of him.

"There it is," she said, pointing into the night sky.

He traced the handle with his eyes, down to the cup, and up, to the north star.

"It's not the brightest star in the sky," he said.

"But it's always there," she said.

"Even when you can't see it," he said.

"I'm awfully tired, of a sudden," she said.

"I won't be here much longer," he said.

"Don't be foolish," she said. "Let's get on home."

"You're right," he said, shivering a bit. "The temperature sure drops with the sun."

Eli took her hand and they stood up .

"Look Eli," Maggie said. "Perfect Tyme. You should bring your watch in tomorrow and have it looked at. I bet they could fix it."

"My watch," Eli said. He hadn't thought of his watch for quite some time. Now, he tried to look through the small glass window of the old clock shop to see what was inside.

"Maybe I will," he said. He tugged Maggie's hand and they headed for home.

CHAPTER NINTEEN

MAGGIE WAS READING a magazine in bed, leaning back against two pillows with the quilted bedspread covering her legs when Eli came out of the bathroom. She quickly put the magazine down on the nightstand, as Eli came out. Eli walked around the front of the bed to his side. He'd gotten used to having a side. He just couldn't always remember which side was his. So it helped when Maggie got in bed first. He knew what to do, when she did. He watched her, out of the corner of his eye, as he came around the bed, trying hard to make like he wasn't watching her. She didn't look at him either, but kept her eyes down, tracing the quilted pattern of the bedspread with her finger. He sat down on the edge of the bed, kicked off his slippers and turned out the light.

In those moments just after losing the light, the darkness almost overwhelmed him. Blindness. Complete. It seemed for an instant that he was not connected to his body. He just was. Or was he. He wasn't sure. Consciousness. He could think, he thought. Everything else was gone. Black. Dizzying blackness.

"Are you alright?" Maggie called from beyond the dark.

Eli held on to the bed. A warm hand touched his back. The light returned, gradually at first, then in abundance. Harvest moonlight danced through the curtains and cracks, filling the room with liquid silver, not to be kept out. "Where was the light a moment ago," Eli thought.

"I'm fine," he whispered.

He swung his feet up, adjusted his body, covered himself with the comforter, and lay down, sinking into the softness of the pillow.

"You sure you're alright?" Maggie said.

A moment passed.

"I'm sure," Eli said, reaching out to her.

He touched her bare arm. It was warm, and soft. She hadn't moved. She was still leaning up against the headboard. He lightly ran his finger up and down the inside of her forearm, feeling the softness of her skin, just below her biceps. She shivered slightly. He felt the roughness of his fingers, against her softness. He took her hand and placed the inside of her wrist against his lips. He could feel her heart beating in his kiss. He caressed her arm with his lips, slowly.

He reached up and touched her cheek, and she turned to him.

She whispered, "Eli, are you..."

"Shssh," he touched her lips with his finger, gently.

Slowly, he felt the moistness of her lips with his finger. She kissed his finger as he softly caressed her mouth. He let his finger slide down her chin. He felt the softness of her neck with his hand. His hand continued downward, floating across the front of her soft cotton nightgown, feeling the rising and falling of her breasts. Her breathing caught, as he touched her, then quickened. His fingers lingered, feeling her softness beneath the thin fabric of nightgown. In the moonlight, he began to feel the pattern. Then gently, ever so gently, he pressed, and held and withdrew. Then pressed again.

"Ohhhhhhh," escaped her as a barely audible breath.

He pulled the loose elastic collar of her nightgown down and kissed her bare shoulder, tenderly. She touched his face with her hand, not seeing his eyes. In feeling his skin, rough and weathered, she knew his eyes were closed. He always closed them. She liked to watch him touch her.

He kissed her neck. She undid the top button of his pajama top and slid her hand inside, feeling the muscles of his chest, still strong and firm. She could feel his muscles rippling with his movement, as her hands found their way to his shoulders, and then his back. He pulled her nightgown down, just a little further, and traced the contour of her soft, tender skin, just above her breast, rising, in the moonlight. His finger dipped beneath the fabric, touching, teasing. She took a quick breath and looked at him, wondering, vulnerable. How did he so completely know her, know what she needed. It had been so long. So very long.

He looked up, as she thought this.

Their eyes met.

Shining.

Moist.

Timeless. And deep.

"I love you," he said.

She smiled. Relieved.

"I knew you would," she said. "Once you got to know me."

Together, they laughed.

He kissed her. She kissed him.

Light, imperceptible light, coalesced around them, in their timeless, and ageless embrace.

CHAPTER TWENTY

WILMA AND A VERY PREGNANT SARAH WERE SELLING JAMS and jellies just as fast as they could, as the Salem Harvest Festival continued into its second and final day. Out of the corner of her eye, Sarah was stealing glances of her Mother and Father, Maggie and Eli. Eli had turned over the Cider Press to Tom and Jaren and was helping Maggie with pies and tarts.

"What's up with Grandpa today," Sarah said to Wilma, in between customers.

"What do you mean?" Wilma said, handing a jar of Spellman Farms Apple Butter to a tourist.

"C'mon Wil. Haven't you been watching?" Sarah expanded. "Just look at them."

Both women paused to stare at Maggie and Eli. Maggie was serving pie and ice cream to customers from behind a folding church table. Eli was helping, sort of. He was touching Maggie constantly. He had has arm around her waist. He moved to her other side, sliding his hand across her back. They held hands, during a break in the action. She rubbed his back. He touched her arm. He changed sides, sliding his hand across her backside, just a little bit too low, in Sarah's opinion. Eli squeezed. Maggie jumped, and giggled.

"Oh my," Wilma said.

"Just like a couple of newlyweds," Sarah said.

Conscious that she was being watched, Maggie turned and winked at her daughters. Both women blushed, and looked away. Maggie just smiled.

"I can't believe it," Sarah said.

"They're acting like kids," Wilma said.

"What are you two girls gabbing about now," Ken said, bringing up a fresh case of apple butter for the women.

"Oh nothing, we're just spying on the love birds," Wilma said.

Ken set the case on the shelf, behind the girls.

"I wouldn't worry about Jaren's new girl friend if I were you, Wilma. She's a good girl," Ken said.

"What girlfriend?" Wilma said, shocked.

Sarah scowled at Ken.

"Did I say girlfriend?" Ken back peddled.

Wilma looked over to the cider press, noticing a cute brown-haired girl standing much too close to her son.

"I didn't mean girlfriend," Ken continued to back up. "I meant to say friend. A girl. Well, she is his friend..."

"Ken," Sarah stopped him. "Be quiet. We were talking about Grandma and Grandpa."

Wilma kept her eyes on her teenage son and the brown-haired girl, as her husband turned the press screw.

"What about them?" Ken said, grateful his wife had got him out of that jam.

"Just look at them," Sarah said.

Ken watched. Wilma reluctantly took her eyes off her son.

"They can't keep their hands off each other," Sarah said. Wilma scowled, thinking more about her son.

Ken watched, with the women for a moment. Maggie fed Eli a bite of pie. She wiped a bit off of his chin, then stuck her finger in his mouth. Eli sucked the pie off her finger.

"Ooooo," Sarah said. "I can't look."

Ken laughed, then grabbed Sarah and pulled her close.

"I hope when I'm their age, I've still got it in me," he said.

He pressed Sarah's very round belly against his, and began to sway to music apparently only he could hear.

"Kenny!" Sarah protested.

He grabbed her arm and twirled her out, then reeled her in, and kissed her deeply, bending to accommodate her rounded condition. Her knees nearly buckled. He held her up and released her. Her eyes were half open, dreamy.

"Kenny!" She cooed.

Wilma fanned herself.

"It's not hard to see how you got to be where you are today," Wilma said, enviously.

Ken let her go. Sarah recovered quickly. Ken put more cases on the shelf.

"But what happened to them," she said. "They're old."

"They're in love," Ken said.

"But they're my parents," she said. "They're not supposed to act like that in public."

"Why not?" Ken said seductively.

He put his arms around Sarah from behind. It was easier, with her basketball front. He kissed the back of her neck. His hands rubbed her belly, then found their way up, to the crease between her belly and her breasts. He lifted his hands up, just a little. Just enough. He smiled, deliciously.

"Just because they're old, doesn't mean they still can't..."

"Kenny, stop that," Sarah said slowly, unconvincingly.

Ken laughed, enjoying the effect he was having on his wife.

"See what I mean," he said. Who'd a thought that you, as far along as you are would still like..."

"Kenny!" Sarah flared, turning bright red.

Sarah looked at Wilma, trying to disguise her embarrassment, hoping her Sister-in-law hadn't seen. Wilma wasn't paying any attention. Relieved, Sarah followed Wilma's gaze, curious to see what had drawn her attention away from their public display of affection. She immediately saw what Wilma was watching so intently. Tom, in his tight levi's and flannel shirt, was spinning the fly wheel of the cider press with a swaying, rhythmic, fluid motion. Jaren turned the press screw as his father put more apples in the hopper. Juice was flowing from the press in abundance. The brown-haired girl watched. Father and Son were working together like a well-oiled machine.

"Help me out here Wilma," Sarah said, testing whether Wilma had actually been distracted.

"What was that?" Wilma said, her voice sounding like it came from someplace other than where she was standing.

Ken saw what Wilma had been looking at and laughed.

"I'll be back in a while," Wilma said, walking away. "You two seem like you can handle it here," giving special emphasis to handle.

Sarah's cheeks flushed deeper.

Ken laughed again, watching Wilma leave. He kissed Sarah's neck.

"See," he said. "It's contagious."

"Kenny," Sarah said, succumbing.

She turned around and kissed him back.

"Say," an older lady said, coming up to the display booth. "What are you folks putting in that apple butter. I'd like to get some for my husband."

Sarah handed the woman a jar. Her cheeks matched the color of the delicious red apple on the label.

CHAPTER TWENTY-ONE

"LET'S GO GET SOME ICE CREAM," Eli said, as Maggie handed a hot apple tart to one of the afternoon visitors.

"Ice cream!" Maggie exclaimed. "We've got a ton of ice cream here."

"Okay, dish me up some, and let's go for a walk," Eli said.

Maggie looked at him a little closer. She could see he was tired. The shadows under his eyes were deepening.

"How about a cone," she said.

"Sounds great," Eli said.

Maggie made him a cone and then took off her Spellman Farms apron.

"Think you can handle things without me Marci?" Maggie asked, hanging her apron up on a peg behind their table. Marci smiled and nodded.

"It's about time," Marci said. "It's nearly impossible to get anything done with you two fooling around most of the time."

"Fine," Maggie huffed, mockingly. "We'll just take our leave then."

Marci laughed. "Have fun," she said, winking at Maggie.

Maggie took Eli's free hand and they walked away.

Hand in hand, Maggie and Eli walked through the displays and booths. This was the big finale of the Harvest Festival. The afternoon crowds were thinning, in anticipation of the evening entertainment. Maggie and Eli walked out of the festival displays, and into the town square.

"Let's sit," Eli said, tiring noticeably.

They sat down and rested, watching the crowds stroll through the Festival displays, from their distant vantage point.

Neither spoke. They found no need to. As the moments passed by peacefully, they could feel each other's thoughts in their simple touch, holding hands. Eli felt the subtle afternoon breeze gently caress his skin. The sun was warm and fading. Maggie was by his side. They had worked hard together. He felt a connection with her, a deep, deep connection. How many trips around the sun had the earth made, since he had known this woman? How many sun rises and sunsets? How many more sunsets would he enjoy with her?

He felt each moment new, in her presence. He could not remember her not being with him, her presence, her touch. Yet, he could not remember the details. Most of his memories were relearned, and relived, through her eyes, and her words, and her touch. She had been patient with him.

What did it all mean? He still hadn't figured it out. But, he had come to accept it—this new life. At least, it seemed like this was his new life. His reborn life. He believed that this life was infinitely better than the nightmare, and it must have been a nightmare, of his former life—the horrible dream life that was so vividly etched in his mind. He had a family now, children, grandchildren. He had a wife, friend, lover. He had it all. There was nothing more he could ask of, or expect of life.

His only regret was that he had not enjoyed the whole of it. There was much that was missing from his memory. And, while he had promised not to speak of it, there was much of his memory he would choose not to have. Nevertheless, he felt gratitude. He felt warmth. He felt peace. He couldn't remember the last time he had felt peaceful. Suddenly, as suddenly as the dew distilling upon the grass on a summer's night, he had peace.

"I brought your watch," Maggie said.

As soft and gentle as her voice was, it shattered his reverie. He had been staring at the sun. He turned to the sound of her voice, but he could not see her.

"What?" he said, disoriented.

"I brought your watch," she said again.

"My watch?" Eli said, trying to make a connection between his thoughts and her words. They didn't connect. He didn't think he could cross the vast river between.

"Perfect Tyme," she said. "Maybe they can fix it."

She held the watch out to him.

He looked at it. He remembered. He didn't want to.

"Oh, that's right," he said.

He took the watch. It was cold to his touch. He shivered.

"Are you alright," she said, worried.

He looked at her. He looked at the watch. He thought, "Time unfolds us."

"I'll be alright," he said, sadly. "Maybe," he thought.

"How 'bout if I pick up a few things at Bock's, for the kids, while you get your watch fixed," she said, feigning enthusiasm.

"Sure," he said, standing up.

"Be right back," she said. She squeezed his hand and left him.

He watched her go, silhouetted against the setting sun. Across the square, a bell tinkled. The toy store swallowed her. He tore his gaze away from the sun. A matching bell tinkled. He stepped into "Perfect Tyme".

A surging rush, a wall of rhythmic, pulsing sound engulfed him as he entered the aging clock shop. Tings, and pings, and gongs. Clicks and ticks and tocks. The sound was everywhere. Cuckoo. Cuckoo. He was drowning. He couldn't breathe. Old museum smells filled his nostrils. He couldn't see. The sound. The sound. His head hurt. His brain pulsed out of rhythm, to every other sound that was out of rhythm. He leaned against a large dark shape. Donggggggg. Donggggggg. The force of the vibration shook him. He staggered deeper and deeper into the darkness. A bit of yellowing light. He could see again, a little. Thousands of clocks. Grandfather clocks. Wall clocks. Table top clocks. Windup clocks. Clocks with exposed innards, twisting and writhing to an asynchronous beat. Tiny clocks. Intricately carved wooden clocks. All covered with a heavy layer of graying dust. Undisturbed. Where did they stop?

"May I help you?" a remarkably vibrant young woman said.

She smiled at him from behind a glass counter, a warm, friendly, encouraging smile. He felt much better.

"My watch," he said. He could breathe again. The rushing torrent had passed. "Can you fix it?" He held it out to her.

She reached her hand out to take the watch from him. She touched his hand. Pain. The pain of frostbite, warming. Deep, deep frostbite. He hadn't realized he was so cold. Frozen. His fingers were frozen. She was so warm. Her fingers touched his hand. Pain. Thawing. His fingers ached, tingled, vibrated with the warmth. Pain. Throbbing. Pulsing. He dropped the watch. It clattered against the glass counter.

"I'm so sorry," she said, ripples creasing the milky skin of her perfect forehead.

He looked at the watch. She looked at the watch.

"It's broken," she said, simply.

"Can you fix it?" he said, annoyed.

She looked up at him. She looked at him. Those eyes. He could see the passage of time, the ticking of every clock, in the endless, aging shop, reflecting in her eyes. He held his breath. She held his watch.

"No," she said.

Breathe. He could breathe. Relief. She smiled. He didn't want it fixed.

He reached for the watch. She turned and vanished behind a dark paneled door.

"Hey, wait!" he called. "My watch!"

He heard the scraping of wood against wood, above the cacophony of clock. His head was hurting again.

She returned, as quickly as she had gone, carrying a small piece of yellowed paper and a brown, dull pencil.

"Put your name and phone number right here," she pointed at the paper and smiled at him. Her smile. He forgot his headache.

He wrote his name and phone number on the yellowed paper, just where she had pointed. He wanted to please her. He wanted her to smile at him.

"What about my watch?" he said. "I thought you said you can't fix it."

"Oh, I can't," she teased. "But my boss can. He can fix anything."

Eli laughed at her pleasant naivete.

"Can he fix me?" he said, joking.

"Maybe," she said, smiling. She winked at him. "Come back in three days."

He laughed again. If he were about 50 years younger, he might find a pretty good reason to visit this clock shop more often. He turned to go. Looming before him was a great old grandfather clock.

"That must have been what I ran into coming into this shop," he thought.

"Say," he called out, turning back to the young woman behind the glass. She was not there. "What is your name?" he called out louder.

She poked her head around the dark wood door. Her smile warmed him from the distance.

"Margaret," she beamed.

Donggggggggg.

The Great Grandfather clock chimed a deep resonant sound.

Donggggggggg.

Eli staggered out of the shop holding his head, so the pain could not escape.

* * *

The glaring red eye stared, penetratingly, from the jagged horizon. Was it open or closed. He couldn't tell. Eli stared back with equal animosity, squinting his eyes to match the sharpened gaze. He could feel the earth beneath him, moving, turning. He was aware, in his very fiber, of its spinning. His whole body was tuned to it. The great eye was closing. He could see, in the lengthening shadows. It would be dark soon.

A bell tinkled, across the square. He looked to the sound. Maggie smiled. The world stopped turning. Her eyes found him. It was enough.

CHAPTER TWENTY-TWO

ELI RESTED COMFORTABLY, IN HIS LIVING room La-Z-Boy. He let his eyes close. He wasn't necessarily tired. It was just so pleasant. The Harvest Festival was over. The family—his family—was gathered for dinner. He had come to realize, and quite liked that wherever and whenever this family gathered, there would be food. He felt reasonably sure they liked to be together. But, he was even more sure that the reason they did, was that they always, always, had food. Reapings of the harvest, as it were.

With his eyes closed, Eli's other senses heightened.

Noise.

Fifteen souls—eight adults—seven children, soon to be eight.

Joyful Noise.

Eli listened to the noise. The children were playing. The women were making dinner. The men were talking.

Maggie was in her element. She directed traffic, marshaled forces, gave orders, refereed disputes, performed first aid, and made dinner—with help, of course. Wilma mashed the potatoes. Marci tossed the salad. Sarah sat on a stool at the kitchen-island, holding her beach-ball stomach, munching on raw carrots and wishing her due date was two weeks sooner than it was. Jenny and Mary and Chloe all helped set the table.

Eli let the smells and the sounds of dinner swell his anticipation. Pot-roast, slow cooked, while the family went to church, made his stomach growl with nearly every breath. Fresh baked bread, hot rolls, still baking, mixed with the sweet, tart, cinnamon smell of the pies, apple, of course. He wondered if he could ever get tired of fresh hot bread, or hot apple pie alamode. The dinner smells were so warm, so strong, so good, he felt he could live on the smell, that is, until his stomach growled again. With the delicious aroma of the pies, he did consider skipping the roast, and going right to dessert.

"Grandpa, would you read me a story," Emy said, climbing onto Eli's lap.

"Emy," Tom said in rebuke. "Let Grandpa rest."

Emy immediately began to climb down.

Eli grabbed the little girl around the waist and held her fast, hugging her to his chest.

"Let her alone. Do you think I'm old, or something?" Eli said gruffly.

Emy giggled.

"Daddy says you're old," Emy said.

"Emy! Watch your tongue," Tom said.

Emy's cheeks turned bright red. So did Tom's.

"I may be getting old," Eli said, with a twinkle in his eye, "but your Daddy's still my son. And he'd better mind what I say."

Emy liked that.

"Come and Eat," Maggie called from the kitchen.

"Now there's the real boss," Eli whispered to Emy. "We'd all better do what she says."

Emy giggled and jumped off of Eli's lap.

"Pull your old Grandpa up," Eli said, reaching out to Emy.

Emy latched onto Eli's arm and gave a tug. Eli groaned and rose from the chair, pretending Emy was helping. When he reached his feet, he swayed a little, feeling a bit light headed. Andy, crashed into him with a lovable bear hug, stabilizing him.

"C'mon Dad," Andy said. "Let's eat."

"Adults in the dinning room, kids in the kitchen," Maggie ordered.

Jenny sat down at the dinning room table, smiling.

"I don't think so," Wilma said.

"Mommmm please," Jenny whined.

"I need you to take care of your cousins," Maggie said, placing a loving hand on Jenny's shoulder.

"Okay Grandma," Jenny shrugged.

Maggie smiled, and squeezed her Granddaughter tightly. Jenny headed to the kitchen, pausing to glare at Jaren, who was privileged enough to stay.

Three couples sat down, two sons, a daughter and their spouses. It seems they automatically knew where to sit. Maggie remained standing near the kitchen entrance. She still had food to serve. Eli looked around the table. The head and foot were still empty. Which was which. He chose the closest. It must be the head. No one said any different.

"Jacob! Joseph! Hush up," Sarah crossly barked at the kitchen. "Time for a blessing." The youngest cousins usually had trouble settling down. Sarah didn't have much room left in her body for patience.

Everyone folded their arms and bowed their heads. Eli looked at Tom and Wilma, Andy and Marci, Sarah and Ken, all with arms folded and heads bowed.

"Salt of the earth," he thought. "Any man would be proud to own them."

Maggie coughed. She looked up from her head-bowed position and nodded at him. He looked back at her, puzzled.

"The blessing," she mouthed.

"What?" he said back to her, out loud.

Everyone at table opened their eyes and looked at him, without changing their reverential position. Giggles poured from the kitchen. Motherly scowls flowed back.

"The prayer. Bless the food," she said.

A shock ran through him. He lost his breath. He shook his head.

"Oh no!" he said, wide eyed. "Someone else can say it." Pangs of fear were shooting through him. Here was family tradition. He knew, deep down, it had special, meaningful significance.

"Bless the food." Maggie's quiet command echoed in his brain, clattering against all the other sensations of wonder he felt at being a part of this family.

"Bless the food." Who was he to pronounce a blessing. He had no authority. He could not bless anyone, or anything.

Tom reached out from his seat, next to Eli and put his left hand on Eli's shoulder.

"You preside, Pop," he said quietly. "We all look to you."

Eli couldn't remember ever saying a prayer. He must have. They expected it. Seeing them, he wanted it. He closed his eyes. He bowed his head. He sat very still. He would try.

"Oh God," he rasped, barely above a whisper.

What next? What should he say? "If there is a God, and if you are God," he thought. Did he say that out loud? He wasn't sure.

He opened his eyes to see if anyone noticed. All eyes were closed. All heads were bowed. Except, for Maggie. She was watching him. Their eyes met. Encouragement.

"Thank you for this harvest," he said. He meant it.

A moment passed. He felt something stir, deep within him. He wasn't sure what it was. He was sure he couldn't speak it. But he knew she was listening.

"And I don't just mean the food," he managed.

His voice caught. Emotions he could never express bridged the spillway of his eyes. He was swimming under water. Everything was blurry. He could feel the flowing current and was caught up in it. He could smell the smells of abundance. He could hear the winds whispering through this family tree. But he could not speak. So deep. So rich. So fulfilled. He closed his eyes. The spillway opened and streaked his cheeks.

"Thank you," he said softly, finally.

He looked up, slowly. All heads were bowed. All eyes were closed. Except hers. Again, their eyes met.

Timeless. Ageless. Eternal. What he wouldn't give to look in those eyes forever.

"Thank you," she mouthed.

Her unspoken words caressed his soul. She smiled. His heart broke.

Sarah opened one eye, to peak. Maggie saw. The spell was broken.

"Amen," Maggie said.

"Amen," they all echoed.

"Let's eat," Jaren said enthusiastically. He reached for the pot-roast before anyone else could get it.

Maggie touched the fabric of her apron to her eyes. Eli wiped moist salt trails from his cheeks. They all began to eat.

CHAPTER TWENTY-THREE

THAT INCESSANT TICKING sound filled his mind. Thousands and thousands of clocks, each keeping their own time, some fast, some slow. Eli walked deeper and deeper into the clock shop. He was looking for Margaret. She had his watch.

Suddenly, an old, wind-up alarm clock, with two bells on top, began to ring. He stopped and looked at it. It was dancing on an old dusty shelf. It kept ringing louder and louder. The vibration caused it to move closer to the edge. It was going to fall off. Eli saved it from falling. He could feel the vibration in his fingers, his hand, his wrist. The ringing vibration traveled down his arm. His whole body was vibrating. He pushed the brass buttons on top of the clock. He had to make it stop. It wouldn't stop. He pushed harder. It wouldn't stop. He held the bells and felt the ringing travel through him. He couldn't stand it. He would be consumed by the sound, by the vibration. He crashed the clock, violently, against the shelf. The glass face shattered. The clock ceased to vibrate. The ringing sound traveled through him and out into the void.

"Eli, wake up!"

Eli felt for the broken clock.

"Eli, Sarah's at the hospital. There's a problem."

Eli sat up in bed. He couldn't hear the ticking.

"Get dressed. They need us." Maggie was already out of bed, putting on her clothes.

Eli swung his legs over the edge of the bed and sat up.

Maggie switched on the light. Eli groaned, covering his eyes. Her light was painfully brilliant. Sarah needed her.

"What time is it?" he asked.

"Two a.m." she said.

* * *

Eli sat in the maternity ward waiting room with his eyes closed. It hurt to keep them open. He could feel the fluorescent lights pulsating with a constant, nauseating, 60-cycle hum. It didn't matter what time it was, day or night, these lights made you look and feel horrible. He rested his head against the wall, as if he were trying to get a radio-active tan from the slightly green, pulsing lights. He was alone. A TV mounted on the wall played late night reruns. He tried to watch, but couldn't. The sound was too low to listen. He tried to fold his legs over the chair next to him, to get comfortable. A black and white clock watched him from the opposite wall, unblinking.

"Move," he demanded.

No response.

His eyes closed.

He heard footsteps in the corridor.

He sat up. He didn't want anyone to think he had been sleeping.

Maggie and Ken came in, looking grim.

"They kicked me out," Ken said. "They won't let me stay with her."

Ken's face looked gray. Eli questioned Maggie with her eyes. Ken collapsed in the chair across from Eli.

"C-section," Maggie said. "Emergency."

"Why?" Eli asked.

"Chord's wrapped around the baby's neck. The heartbeat dropped way too low."

"Sarah's blood pressure was awfully low too," Ken said.

Maggie looked at Eli and nodded.

"They don't mess around," Maggie said.

She sat down next to Eli and grasped his hand. They all sat, stunned into silence, waiting.

Waiting.

With Maggie near, Eli was not so concerned about staying awake. He closed his eyes, again.

"Mr. Chapman?"

"Who's that?" Eli thought. His eyes snapped open. His stomach had that interrupted-sleep nausea feeling. His head hurt. He remembered. The room was the same. The clock kept changing. He must have slept.

A maternity nurse wearing flower print magenta scrubs had startled them. The magenta print was fighting with the green fluorescence for dominance. It made him dizzy. Eli thought the fluorescence won. Ken stood up. Maggie stood up. Eli stood up, slowly.

"Mr. Chapman," the nurse repeated. "Your wife is fine. They gave her an epidural, so she was awake for the entire procedure. She would like to see you."

Ken and Maggie and Eli breathed out a collective sigh of relief. But, their breath was sucked into the vacuum of unspoken words. Maggie gasped.

"What about the baby?"

Ken's eyes were wild. He advanced on the nurse. She tried to retreat. He grabbed her arms.

"Your baby is in critical condition," she stiffened in Ken's captivity.

He shrank from the weight of her words.

She backed away.

"The doctors are working with your baby now," she said. "Your wife needs you."

Her words commanded him to follow. He did. Maggie and Eli collapsed into the waiting room chairs, void of more information.

The hands of the clock spun out of control.

"What time is it, really?" Eli thought.

* * *

For the next several days, the clock continued to move, but time did not.

"It's a girl," they said, with an uncomfortable smile.

Sarah suffered the physical pains of surgical recovery. Her body was healthy. She would heal quickly. By day two, the evil nurses had forced her to walk the halls. She thought her stitches would rip and her insides would come tumbling out. It would serve them right.

Her spirit, tied intimately to the tiny body in ICU, might not heal so fast. Bone of her bones, flesh of her flesh, the tiny life which had danced within her for many months, had been torn from her belly at the point of a knife and not returned to her breast. If she would see this fragile soul, she must dawn the equalizing garb of a clean room drone. At best, her time with her baby, Esther—that was Ken's idea—Sarah called her Essy—was limited.

Meconium aspiration. Damaged lungs. Pneumonia. Let's see what develops. She knew these doctors needed more practice.

Sarah held the tiny girl and wept, the day they made her go home. She wouldn't leave her baby there. She wouldn't. She couldn't. Essy screamed. She pulled the cruel IV from her head. They rammed it back in. She pulled it out. They shaved a new spot of long black hair and stabbed her again. Stop it. Just stop. She sobbed uncontrollably. Ken held her. Maggie watched, through the glass, as the whitened figures put the naked, tiny body back in the incubator rack.

Ken pushed her out the door in a squeaky wheel chair. Maggie carried her things. "Ironic," Sarah thought. "They make me walk the halls, and then won't let me walk out the door."

"GIVE ME BACK MY BABY," she screamed inside her head.

Eli was waiting out front of the hospital, in the Chapman's mini-van. Ken opened the side door. Sarah climbed in, wincing, silently. Maggie got in front. Ken got in back. Eli drove home.

CHAPTER TWENTY-FOUR

TIME SEEMED TO HAVE STOPPED FOR ELI. The world hung in the balance, weighed against the tiny body of a fragile baby girl. Days were exhausting.

Lunches to make.

School.

Soccer practice.

Piano lessons.

The twins.

The family pitched in to help Sarah and Ken. Eli watched with exhausted amazement. How did Maggie do it? He was tired, just helping. Had she done this forever?

Maggie and Eli watched the boys during the day. Wilma and Marci took them after school. Sarah stayed at the hospital, for as long as they would let her. Maggie and Wilma and Marci would take turns, holding and feeding the baby, when they could convince Sarah to rest.

Nights were frightening.

Dreams.

Visions.

Ghosts.

Memories.

Rest was impossible. The medical bills were unbelievable. Ken was consumed. Sarah was obsessed. The strength of weak ties kept them going. Breathe in. Breathe out.

Eli stood outside the neo-natal unit as the shifts were changing. Maggie was inside, holding and rocking

Essy. That's what everyone called her now. The nurses had vanished. Eli watched Maggie, through the glass. He could see so much love. She was so tender. So good. His heart ached for Sarah and Ken. His body hurt for this little baby. His stomach got queasy when he thought about the terrible trouble they had with the IV.

Maggie motioned to him.

"Come in," he read her lips.

Eli looked around. No nurses. He pressed the metal safety bar and the neo-natal ICU doors clanged open. He stepped inside. He felt the rush of air chill his ears, as the pressure difference between the inside and outside squished to equalize. The doors closed with a sucking hiss.

"Gown up," he heard Maggie call, from the inner sanctum.

He put on the paper like clean room garb, pants, shirt, cap, booties and gloves. He opened the inner door and went to Maggie's side.

She smiled.

"She's beautiful," Eli said. "Except for the patchwork hair style."

"Those doctors ought to be shot," Maggie said, reverently. She gently stroked Essy's head. There wasn't much hair left.

"How is she?" Eli asked.

"She's doing great," Maggie said. "She's gaining weight. Her oxygen count is good. I think they are just being extra cautious. Here, you take her."

Maggie carefully stood up.

"Oh no," Eli protested. "You..."

Maggie handed the baby to Eli.

"I've got to go to the bathroom," she said.

Eli took the tiny infant in his arms. Maggie rushed out. "She must really have to go," Eli thought. He sat down in the rocking chair. Essy watched him carefully, penetratingly. It seemed like she was really looking at him.

"I know," he said. "I bet you're wondering who I am."

A nurse materialized to scowl at him. He scowled back, lovingly.

"Join the club," he said to Essy.

Eli placed a tiny bottle in her mouth. Essy sucked hungrily. She closed her eyes. Eli watched her carefully. She had a rounded nose, long dark eyelashes, pink chubby cheeks. He rubbed the little white newborn bumps on her forehead and nose. She fussed. He stopped. She was such a tiny, soft, helpless bundle, peaking out from the pink and white hospital wrap. "Where did she come from?" Eli wondered. She was warm. He was glad. The rocking chair squeaked in rhythm to her tiny sucking sounds.

"Hi Dad. Where's Grandma?" Sarah watched him, smiling, in her featureless ICU outfit.

Eli slowly looked up.

"She had to go," he whispered. "Essy's sleeping."

"I'll take her," Sarah said, possessively.

Eli handed Essy to Sarah and stood up. He felt cold, as he let her go. Sarah sat down with Essy cradled close to her chest. Eli turned to go. The ICU nurse seemed pleased.

"Oh, Dad," Sarah said.

Eli turned around.

"Ken said somebody called about your watch."

Eli froze. He could suddenly smell isopropyl alcohol and betadyne antiseptic. He felt sick. He looked around for something to hold onto. There wasn't anything.

"My watch?" he said.

"Yeah. They said it's ready."

Eli could see Maggie through the wire-reinforced glass of the ICU window. The warmth of her smile was trapped on the other side of the glass. He looked at Sarah and Essy and remembered the warm spot, against his chest where the baby used to be.

"Thanks," he said.

"Love you," she said.

Her words washed over him like a cool shower. He felt goosebumps rise beneath his scrubs.

CHAPTER TWENTY-FIVE

ELI STOOD IN FRONT OF THE DOOR to Perfect Tyme. It had begun to rain. "So much for Indian summer," he thought. It was a cold rain. He was getting wet. He tried to see inside the shop. The small glass opening in the door window was dark. He hesitated. They had his watch. He remembered the pain from last time. He didn't want it. He turned the tarnished brass handle and went in. The tiny bell tinkled as the door opened. He waited for the wall of sound to bury him. He listened, expecting, anticipating the ticking of all the clocks that ever were. It was silent.

Perfect silence.

The aging Grandfather Clock stood sentry, motionless. The gnarled hands were frozen, covering its face. The great, golden pendulum hung in stillness.

Heavy silence. Beating heart.

Eli looked for other clocks, for signs of life. Nothing. The clocks were still there. The dust was still there. The old museum smells were still there. But the ticking was not. Not one single clock was ticking. It was as if each had taken rest, with hands in different positions, at the same moment. Eli wanted to run. He could not. He drifted deeper into the shop on the silent current. The same yellowing light cast odd shaped shadows. There was a body at the glass counter. A smallish man with a green jewelers visor peered through a magnifying reticule at something, Eli couldn't tell what.

He couldn't see the man's eyes. The man did not appear to notice Eli. Eli walked up to the counter. The man continued his work. Eli could see now, that the man was working on a watch, a very tiny watch. Eli watched his hands move. His fingers were old and twisted, brownish, with age spots discoloring the already leathered skin. Yet, the fingers were nimble. They moved with re-markable ease. He seemed to be able to reach inside the tiny time-piece and extract the broken parts. "Could he fix it?" Eli wondered.

"Of course I can fix it," the old man said, placing a small spring inside the little instrument.

The old man peered at Eli from under the visor. Green light cut across the bridge of his nose.

"Fix what?" Eli recoiled. "Was he talking about this watch, or his watch?"

The old man went back to his work. Small parts were removed. Small parts were repaired. His twisted fingers snapped the back of the diminutive watch closed and the old man looked up, raising his visor and pulling back the reticule.

Now Eli could see his eyes.

"The question is, Mr. Spellman," Alden Blethen said. "Do you want me to fix it?"

"You!" Eli nearly shouted.

Any remnants of the stale, musty air that filled the old shop had just been sucked out of the room. Eli struggled for breath. He gasped for air.

"Take this little watch, for instance," Mr. Blethen continued. "I happen to know that the owners desperately want it back." Blethen held the tiny watch in his wrinkled palm. Eli felt drawn to look closer.

"This has not been an easy case. The damage is not severe, but the parts are small. My eyesight is not what it used to be. My fingers are knotted."

Eli listened to the old man's voice. It was not a harsh voice. Neither was it a loud voice. He had trouble remembering why he was there.

Blethen closed his twisted fingers over the tiny time-piece and placed it in a manila envelope. He folded the envelope in half and gently tucked it inside a drawer, under the counter.

"My watch," Eli recalled. "Someone called."

"Ah yes," Blethen spoke. "That would have been Margaret." The old man worked his wrinkled self off the counter-stool and ambled into the back room.

"That must have been quite some time ago," Blethen chuckled.

Even though he was in the back room, Eli could hear him perfectly. His words were penetrating.

"Margaret is no longer with us," Blethen said.

Eli felt stung, struck at the heart. Blethen's words were heavy and sharp.

"Not yet," Eli thought. "It can't be." His heart was beating faster. He could feel it in his temples.

Eli heard papers rustling, wood scraping.

"Here it is," Blethen muttered.

The old man emerged from the back, smiling. He was carrying a folded, faded, wrinkled, manila envelope. He set it on the counter. It clanked against the glass top. There was something heavy inside.

Eli looked down at the folded envelope. Blethen looked down at the folded envelope.

"Open it," Eli thought.

Blethen touched the envelope with his ancient, tree-branch fingers. He unfolded the envelope. There were more folds.

"Do you want to know what's inside?" Blethen spoke. Eli heard him, faintly.

"My watch," Eli thought.

Blethen turned over another fold of the envelope.

"Time does not change us," he said. The old man looked at Eli.

"Yes it does," Eli said. "It does." Eli felt like shouting.

The old man opened another fold.

"Do you want it fixed?" Blethen asked.

"I thought it was," Eli said.

"Not yet," Blethen said.

"I've changed," Eli pled.

Blethen looked at Eli. Eli could feel his eyes, inside him.

"Just unfold it," Blethen said, pushing the envelope across the glass counter. Eli opened the last fold. The old man smiled. Eli felt this smile cutting at his heart. Blethen tore open the dried-out old envelop and took out a watch. Eli's golden watch. He held it in the palm of his weathered hand.

"Isn't it beautiful," Blethen said. "A long time ago, my father purchased a number of these watches. Each one was specially inscribed. He paid a great price."

Blethen opened the gold watch, revealing the crystal face and inside cover.

"My watch?" Eli thought.

"For you," Blethen said.

Eli looked at the watch. The crystal face was perfect. He could not see the engraving inside. He was reluctant to touch it.

"Take it, if you will," the old man invited. "You've paid the price."

"I have?" Eli said.

Slowly. Ever so slowly. Eli reached his hand out and touched the watch. The old man closed his wrinkled fingers, holding Eli's hand. The watch face snapped shut, sandwiched between their palms.

The room shifted. He felt the dusty floor move beneath his feet. The world was turning.

Dongggggggg.

Tick, tick, tick.

Tock.

Tick, tick, tick.

Tock.

Dongggggggg.

Clang. Cuckoo. Cuckoo.

Every clock in the shop was ticking. The sound overwhelmed him. Dizzy. Falling.

Dongggggggg.

The old man still held his hand. He could feel the watch, between them. The cold metal grew warm, warmer, hot, hotter. Heat. Pain. Burning. The old man smiled.

"It's time," he said.

Dongggggggg.

Eli could feel his words inside his chest, above, and beneath the rhythmic clatter of countless clocks.

Donggggggggg.

The old man released his grip. Eli held the watch in his hand. The old man's hand was open still. Eli opened the watch. There was no engraving inside.

"This isn't my watch," he said. "I don't want it."

"It is," Blethen said.

The old man held his hand up, palm forward. The weathered flesh contained a circular indent, where the watch used to be. Etched, burned, written in the center of his hand, Eli could read the words:

Elijah Spellman. Time does not...

The old man closed his fist. Eli staggered from the blow.

Donggggggggg.

The clocks were beating in his brain.

Donggggggggg.

He felt the watch, now cool inside his own palm.

Donggggggggg.

He had to get out of there.

Donggggggggg.

He staggered back, away from the counter. The old man smiled, sadly.

Donggggggggg.

He passed the great Grandfather clock. The pendulum was swinging, forward, then back.

Donggggggggg.

Eli pulled open the shop door. The tiny bell tinkled. The sound was lost among the ticking clocks. Eli staggered out the door, into the rain. He heard the great Grandfather clock toll once more, as the shop door closed. He reeled from the sound. Across the square, he was saved. Maggie stood, umbrella in hand, smiling, waiting. He would go to her. He stepped off the curb.

"Why was it so far down today?" he thought, vertigo seizing him. "Would he never reach the street?" Falling. Falling. The wet pavement glistened as the headlights flashed by. He misjudged his distance, badly. His ankle hit the ground and turned over. Eli winced in pain and crashed to the street. His head hit the pavement. White flashes shot through his field of vision. The world was swirling in a drowning vortex.

Distantly, he heard a woman scream.

"Maggie," he thought.

The smell of diesel exhaust filled his nostrils.

Red flashes joined the white flashes pulsing inside his head.

A siren chirped, twice.

Eli opened his eyes.

Maggie," he croaked.

His head was on the ground, cold. He could see a small stream, growing, flowing amidst the gutter sand-bars, towards a distant storm drain. Bright lights were coming. Red lights were going. Tear drops were falling.

"Make way."

"It took you long enough."

"When'd it happen?"

"Twenty minutes ago. I gotta schedule to keep."

"Not today."

Poking. Prodding. Eli rolled over, involuntarily. His arms were yanked out of his coat.

"Are you O.K?"

"Maggie," he answered.

Bright lights pierced his eyes. Something stung his forehead. His arm was being squeezed.

"Got an ID?"

"Spellman. Lives right here, upstairs."

A short fat man stood in the stairwell of a dirty old building. He was chewing on a cigar.

"No, it can't be." His mind was screaming. His voice was silent. His body was shaking.

"Hold still old man. We'll take care of you."

"Maggie," he called.

"BP 90 over 70."

"Heart rate, 140."

"Call Seattle General. We better get him in quick."

"Seattle General." "No." He knew it. "No." In a flash, it all came back. "No. No. Noooooooooooo."

"Maggie," he wept.

It was a dream. It had been a dream. It seemed so real. He really was alone. He couldn't bare it."

"Who's Maggie?"

Eli tried to answer. A collar closed around his neck. He couldn't speak. He couldn't move his head. He couldn't breathe.

"One, two, three."

"Augh!" Eli was jolted and moved.

"ETA, 15 minutes."

"My watch," he cried. He tried to move his head. He tried to speak. This was not his life. He would not have it.

"Maggie! My watch."

Where was it? He couldn't find it. It burned him. His palm. He remembered. His fingers were clenched. He felt it. Still there. Can't see it. He struggled.

"Hold still old man."

Struggle. He lifted his arm. It was heavy, oh so heavy.

"Strap him in."

Convulsing.

He could see it. The gold watch was glistening in the dampness of his palm. He opened the watch face. It was perfect. It was time.

Ziiiiiiiiiiiip. A strap captured his leg. He kicked out with his other.

"Grab him."

"Give me a hand."

He twisted violently. Back and forth. Back and forth.

"He's crazy."

Back and forth.

"Look out!"

Falling.

"Maggie!"

"Ooof." He hit the ground, hard.

His head hurt. His lungs hurt. His body hurt. His heart hurt. The white flashes in his eyes were more insistent.

"Grab him, damn it. Strap him down."

"Here, use this."

"Ouch." A bee stung his shoulder.

"Get him back on the gurney."

"No," Eli said. He looked at the golden watch. It was keeping perfect time. He raised it up. A moment passed. Not long. He brought it down, violently. The crystal face shattered against the rain-dampened pavement. The fragments glistened in the shifting light. Again, he hammered the ground with the fragile time piece. The hands broke off. Again, and again. He felt the earth beneath him.

Spinning.

Slowing.

Stopping.

Stopped.

He closed his eyes. The bright light shown through, pink. The smell of apple blossoms filled the air.

* * * * *

ABOUT THE AUTHOR

OVER THE PAST 20 YEARS, JAMES DALRYMPLE has written, produced, directed and edited television commercials, films, videos and multi-media projects. He currently owns and operates a production/post production studio featuring state of the art technology. He has worked as a writer, producer, director, editor and director of photography on numerous film and broadcast projects, including: *Behind the Academy Awards*, a tv special for Associated Television International; television and radio commercials for Time-Warner, TransAmerica, Glendale Federal Bank, In-Touch Communications; films for Saab, Mazda, Honda, Bandai Toys, Mattel Toys; and, visual effects for *Border Town*, a sci-fi fantasy pilot. Mr. Dalrymple has recently completed a feature-length screenplay titled, *The Mourning Dove*, based on a best selling novel by Larry Barkdull. The screenplay has been approved for production and Mr. Dalrymple has been slated to direct.

Mr. Dalrymple was married to the late Marla Maxwell and is the father of 8 children. He is now married to Anne Hanna and together they have 10 children. They reside in Glendora, California.

MORE FROM LIGATT

If you liked THE WATCH then you will love PHANTOM WITNESS, another great book from LIGATT Publishing. In book stores everywhere.

PHANTOM WITNESS
by Michael B. Druxman

While running from the law in Dallas, small-time hustler Charlie Powers is hit by a car and "dies." Clinically dead, he has an out-of-body experience in which he witnesses a still unsolved gangland slaying that took place almost thirty years earlier. And, he recognizes the killer. Brought back to life by paramedics, Charlie pursues an investigation to prove to himself that he really saw what he saw. His quest brings him into conflicts with hot-tempered rednecks, a ruthless Mob boss and corrupt political figures. Unfortunately, everybody he talks to thinks he's delusional... except the killer. This is a violent, fast-moving, edge-of-the-seat thriller.

ISBN: 0-0-9745611-3-4
Retail Price $15.95
Ordering: LIGATT Publishing
                          13428 Maxella Ave.
                          Suite 293
                          Marina Del Rey, CA 90292
                          (866) 3-LIGATT
                          www.ligattpublishing.com

MORE FROM LIGATT

The ultimate motivational tool is now available from Ligatt Publishing. Play the Game and take command of your destiny with:

SET-4-LIFE
THE DIARY OF A CHAMPION
by George B. Thompson

Do You Ever Feel Like You Should Be Further Along With Your Life? How often have you told yourself that you will get out of debit this year? Or that you will spend more time with your loved ones? Or that you will finally get in shape? Why does it never happen?

The answer: DESIRE, FOCUS, ACCOUNTABILITY and CONSISTENCY... the 4 Dimensions of The Set-4-Life! Game which will show you how to achieve more in 90 days than most people do in a year...or NEVER! By playing this game, you learn how to top into a powerful understanding of your true potential as the Champion God designed you to be...and you will have fun along the way...Set-4-Life will change your life.

ISBN: 0-9785328-0-5
Retail Price $19.95
Ordering: LIGATT Publishing
                   13428 Maxella Ave.
                   Suite 293
                   Marina Del Rey, CA 90292
                   (866) 3-LIGATT
                   www.ligattpublishing.com

Printed in the United States
61021LVS00004B/349-465